I0673298

The Collected Supernatural and Weird Fiction of Lettice Galbraith

The Collected Supernatural and Weird Fiction of Lettice Galbraith

Seven Short Stories of the Strange and Unusual Including 'The Blue Room' and 'A Ghost's Revenge'

Lettice Galbraith

LEONAUR

The Collected
Supernatural and Weird
Fiction of
Lettice Galbraith
Seven Short Stories of the Strange and Unusual
Including 'The Blue Room' and 'A Ghost's Revenge'
by Lettice Galbraith

FIRST EDITION

Leonaur is an imprint of Oakpast Ltd

Copyright in this form © 2021 Oakpast Ltd

ISBN: 978-1-915234-36-0 (hardcover)
ISBN: 978-1-915234-37-7 (softcover)

http://www.leonaur.com

Publisher's Notes

Contents

"The Case of Lady Lukestan"

Coeval with the existence of mankind has existed the belief in ghosts. Like other cults, it has had its ups and downs; its periods of exaltation and of persecution.

It has received the sanction of the priesthood and attained the dignity of a special office in the Book of Common Prayer. It has been lashed by the scorn of the materialist, and derided by professors of exact Science. Advancing education stripped it to the skeleton as Superstition, and Advanced Thought has reclothed it with the nebulous draperies of Esoteric Philosophy.

The swing of the pendulum and the exertions of the Society for Psychical Research have improved the position of the ghost, but its rights as a citizen have yet to be established. The State recognises it not. Legally, a ghost labours under greater disadvantages than a Catholic before the passing of the Emancipation Bill. It cannot make a will or bring an action at law. It may not, whatever its qualifications during life, celebrate a marriage or give a certificate of death. No judge on the bench would convict on the evidence of a ghost, though, could *subpoenas* be served on the spirit world, some had escaped the gallows and many died publicly on the scaffold, instead of decently in their beds.

Rightly or wrongly, however, the law takes no cognisance of ghosts, and ghosts would seem to be aware of this and occasionally act with the irresponsibility of those who cannot be called to account.

Legally a ghost has no existence. This point was established in the case of "Lukestan v. Lukestan and others."

The trial, as may be remembered (it was very inadequately reported in the daily papers), involved the succession to the Earldom of Marylebone (1776 G.B.). Mr. Baron Collings, before whom the case was tried, ruled there was no evidence of a legal marriage between the late Lord Lukestan and Miss Pamela Ardilaun, that the entry of the said marriage in the parish register was a forgery, and he directed the jury to give their verdict for the defendants, with costs.

I do not pretend to criticise the learned judge's attitude in the matter, though it was apparent from the first that his "summing-up" was dead against the plaintiff. I merely place before such of the public as may be interested therein the exact facts of one of the most singular cases ever heard in a court of law, and the public, which is always intelligent (is not *vox populi, vox Dei* an all but universally accepted axiom today ?), may judge for itself whether Lady Lukestan, otherwise known as Miss Ardilaun, was entitled to the sympathy due to a deeply injured woman, or the contumely which is justly heaped on the head of an unsuccessful adventuress.

Morally, Miss Ardilaun was not entirely innocent. She undoubtedly played with the feelings of a nervous and hyper-sensitive man. Other women have done the same without any very serious result. The mistake in Miss Ardilaun's case was, that she did not take the trouble to study the mechanism of her plaything. The truth is, that years of overwork, enforced solitude, and rigorous self-repression had reduced the Rev. Cyprian Martyn to a condition of mind closely bordering on insanity, and in this condition, he construed an ordinary flirtation into a cardinal sin.

He believed that in falling in love with Miss Ardilaun and acquainting her with the fact, he had broken his faith with God and man, and incurred the curse pronounced on those who, "having put their hand to the plough, turn back."

In a moment of delirium he told the girl that his choice lay between the Creator and the creature—between Good and evil—and that he had deliberately, and with his eyes open, chosen the latter; that he was prepared to risk all penalties here and pains hereafter for the gratification of his passion; and as he had proved himself unworthy of the high office of the priesthood, he would resign his cure, marry her, and claim the privileges he had purchased at the price of his very soul.

It is at all times dangerous to disclose the inmost workings of the heart to a woman, who rarely comprehends, and can never realise, the length, breadth, and depth of a man's passion, and this mad avowal was the seal of Cyprian Martyn's fate.

Miss Ardilaun probably resented the position assigned her by the terms of her lover's choice. She certainly thought him insane, and the event proved her to be absolutely correct. She very curtly stated that, at no period of their very informal acquaintance, had she reckoned on him as a factor in her future life. She had tolerated his attentions solely because she was bored to distraction in the rural solitude periodically insisted on by her aristocratic and tyrannical invalid aunt; and as to her marriage, the only part he could possibly take in the ceremony would be that of marrying her to another man, for she should never dream for a moment of marrying him. With this rather cruel speech, Miss Ardilaun would have parted from her clerical admirer, but before she could realise his intention, Martyn had caught her in his arms and kissed her passionately, full on the mouth. "You have ruined me body and soul," he said, when at last he released her; "but remember, I *shall* marry you, if not to myself, then to another man. Living or dying I will have my revenge."

This was his farewell. A week later he was found dead in his study, with an empty bottle, which had contained morphia, lying on the table at his side.

That the unhappy man had deliberately taken his own life was beyond a doubt. All his affairs had been set in order, his liabilities paid, and his correspondence and diaries destroyed. He had written to his brother and only near surviving relative, requesting him to receive such goods as he might die possessed of, and begging him to carry out certain directions as to the disposal of his body.

The letter, which was produced at the inquest, also referred to some unpardonable sin committed by the writer, which rendered him unfit for prolonged existence. As the dead man had borne the most exemplary character, and was universally respected, this allusion was generally regarded as a symptom of mental derangement.

The local practitioner stated in evidence that the deceased had consulted him professionally before starting on his annual holiday. He was then in a very low, nervous state, and complained of depression and insomnia. He (the medical man) attributed his condition to over-work and insufficient nourishment. Mr. Martyn was a strict Anglican, and held extreme views on matters of self-discipline. Hallucination as to the commission of some unpardonable sin was a common and painful feature in cases of religious mania, from which, in his (Dr. Garrod's) opinion, the deceased was undoubtedly suffering at the time of his death.

The jury brought in a verdict of "Suicide whilst of unsound mind," and the unfortunate man was buried in the shadow of the village church which for ten dreary years had been the scene of his ministrations.

All this happened in the autumn of 1886. During the following winter I made the acquaintance of Miss Ardilaun at a crowded "At Home" given by the wife of a legal luminary of the first magnitude. She was kind enough to give me a dance, and inquired if I knew many people. I confessed I was practically a stranger, brought by my cousin and particular chum, Charley Roskill, who as a dancing man and a rising "junior" was a *persona gratissama* with his hostess.

I think it was then Miss Ardilaun owned to being tired and suggested that, as the rooms were hot and overcrowded (which was certainly true), we should find a seat outside, and she selected one immediately opposite the stairs.

Our conversation turned chiefly on Roskill, in whom my companion appeared to take more than a little interest. She said Sir Charles had spoken of him as an attorney-general of the future, and she asked what struck me as rather a singular question.

"Is he," she said, "the sort of man to whom you would advise a woman to go if she were in urgent need of assistance and advice?"

I replied, "I was convinced that Roskill, like myself, would at any time be ready to place his entire professional resources at Miss Ardilaun's service, and that he was undoubtedly clever."

She laughed a little. "I wasn't sure," she said; "but you ought to know."

Then she went away on the arm of a young man, who had arrived to claim his partner.

It was Lord Lukestan. I saw them several times in the course of the evening, always sitting out in sheltered corners, and engaged in earnest conversation. Lukestan was a good-looking boy, a year or two Miss Ardilaun's junior, and it struck me that she accepted his manifest admiration in a serious manner, which indicated that she meant business.

I mentioned this to Roskill as we walked home together, and he laughed the suggestion to scorn. Lukestan's people would never permit such a match. It was well known that old Lord Marylebone destined his nephew for his cousin, Lady Adeliza Skelton. It was quite possible that the boy himself might prefer Miss Ardilaun as a bride-elect, but he could not afford to run counter to his uncle's wishes. He was dependent on his prospects as Lord Marylebone's heir, and more than half the property was unentailed.

"Besides," he concluded, "the girl hasn't a penny. She is virtually the companion and white slave of her aunt, old Lady Catermaran. Take my word, it's only a common or garden flirtation, and it won't last long at that."

Roskill speaks with authority on social matters, and I let the subject drop, but somehow, I wasn't convinced.

People talked a good deal about Miss Ardilaun that winter, but with the new season interest in her seemed to die down. She was seldom seen, and I heard, through Roskill, that she was devoting herself entirely to her aunt, who had become a confirmed invalid, and went nowhere. It seemed a dreary life for a young and beautiful woman, and I wondered whether Lord Lukestan's engagement to his cousin, which had been formally announced in all the Society papers, had anything to do with the girl's sudden retirement from the world.

In June Lord Marylebone died. For the past six months he had been hovering on the brink of the grave, and no one had expected him to last so long. He was, from all accounts, a very disagreeable old gentleman, and I should doubt if any of his relatives, even including his only daughter, much regretted his removal to another sphere.

Lukestan attended the funeral as chief mourner, and was present at the subsequent reading of the will. There were a few legacies to servants and dependents, and a suitable provision for Lady Adeliza. The bulk of the property went with the title.

Lukestan was now Lord Marylebone, and a free agent, but the dead man's shoes, for which he had waited, were destined to be fitted on dead man. He left Marylebone Castle for town on the evening of the funeral, an evening made memorable by the occurrence of the worst railway disaster of recent years. The night mail from the North collided with a goods train a-little beyond Settringham Junction, and while the confusion and dismay, incidental to such a misfortune, were at their height, the Lowton and Wolds express dashed into the rear of the wrecked passenger train, and completed a scene of horror rarely equalled in the annals of modern travel.

The daily papers chronicled in full the ghastly details of the catastrophe. The boiler of the express engine burst within a few minutes of the second collision, and steam and fire alike wreaked their fury on the unhappy passengers imprisoned in the overturned carriages. First on the long list of victims, published by the evening press, was the name of Lord Lukestan.

The compartment which had been reserved for his use was reduced to matchwood, and it was only after immense exertions on the part of the officials that the bodies of the young man and his valet could be removed from the mass of smoking debris.

"Poor fellow!" said Roskill, as he put down the paper. "His luck has come too late. I wonder"—he paused to light his cigarette over the lamp—"how Miss Ardilaun will take it?"

We had dined early, preparatory to looking in at the Frivolity, but somehow the smash on the Great Northern had taken the edge off our interest in the new burlesque. Roskill's acquaintance with Luke-stan had been of the slightest; to me he was hardly more than a name, but the tragic circumstances attending his death evoked a sympathy that was almost personal.

"I wonder," Charley repeated, meditatively, "how Miss Ardilaun will take it?"

The words were barely past his lips when the servant appeared with a message.

"Lady to see you, sir. She wouldn't give her name, but I was to say her business was most urgent."

She must have followed close on Stevens's heels, for before he had finished speaking she was in the room. A tall, slender woman, wrapped from head to foot in a long cloak of softly rustling silk. She wore a thick veil, but even under this disguise I was struck by something familiar in her gait and carriage.

The moment the door had closed upon the retreating man, she lifted the thick folds of black gauze. It was Miss Ardilaun. Her eyes were red with weeping, and her face as white as a sheet.

"I hope you will forgive me for disturbing you at this hour," she said, going straight to Charley, "but I knew you lived in chambers, and I wanted to find you at home. I am in great trouble, Mr. Roskill, dreadful trouble, and I must have advice without delay. I thought—I felt sure you would help me."

If Roskill was surprised (and I think he was) he did not show it. He said simply, "I shall be very glad to give you any assistance in my power, Miss Ardilaun," and looked at me.

She followed the direction of his eyes, and became aware, for the first time, of the presence of a third person. I intimated my readiness to withdraw, but she cut me short.

"Please don't go, Mr. Bryant. I am not sure that I don't require a solicitor's rather than counsel's opinion—at present. In any case you may as well hear my story—if you do not mind."

I was only too glad of the opportunity, for I own my curiosity was a good deal excited. We sat down and waited.

Miss Ardilaun's manner was that of a woman who has nerved herself to go through anything. She was unnaturally, almost horribly, calm. She began without any hesitation, speaking in a dry, metallic tone, which was devoid of the least trace of emotion.

"You have seen in the papers that Lord Lukestan was killed last night in the railway accident? I had better tell you at once that he was my husband. We were married last January. There were strong reasons for keeping the marriage secret. Lord Lukestan was entirely dependent on his uncle, who had other views for him, and he dare not risk the consequences of openly disregarding those wishes. At that time Lord Marylebone was not expected to live more than a few weeks, and *he* (Arthur) felt sure that a private marriage would be the easiest way of extricating ourselves from the many family difficulties which surrounded us.

"We never anticipated the necessity for secrecy lasting so long. Of course, Lord Marylebone's partial recovery placed us in a most painful position, but we knew it could only be temporary, and we resolved to chance it and wait. That was why Lord Lukestan's engagement to his cousin was formally announced. What would have happened if the old earl had insisted on their immediate marriage I don't know; fortunately, or unfortunately, he did not make a point of that, and when circumstances rendered it necessary. that our marriage should be acknowledged, Lord Marylebone died. I cannot tell you how rejoiced I was to receive the news, and only last night I went down on my knees and thanked God for this."

She drew a telegram from her pocket and laid it on the table before us. The message had been handed in at Marfleet, the post town for Marylebone Castle, and ran—

Thank Heaven, all right at last, am leaving by night mail. Shall be with you eleven tomorrow. Will see Craike on way. Arthur.

"I thought my prayers had been answered," she went on, in the same low, even voice, "that my troubles were over; but you see I was premature in my thanksgivings. Today I am in the most horrible position in which any woman could be placed—a widow who has never been acknowledged as a wife. I have neither father nor mother. My aunt has never desired my confidence; she has always regarded me in the light of an unpaid servant, and even if I wished to do so, I could not consult her now, for the doctors inform me that in her present state of health any sudden shock might prove fatal. I have no other relations, no one to whom I can turn for help. I *must* make my mar-

13

riage public. What am I to do?"

The first step was manifestly to procure the necessary proofs of the marriage. We said so and inquired whether she was provided with a copy of the certificate.

She replied she was quite certain that no such document had been given or demanded.

"I know nothing about the preliminary arrangements," she said, "I left them entirely to Lord Lukestan. I cannot even tell you the name of the village where we were married, though I should be able to find my way there. It is a tiny place, quite out of the world, about ten miles from Garstang Junction. Parker, Lord Lukestan's confidential servant, met us there with a cart and we drove straight to the church. It stands above the village on the top of a hill. We were married by the vicar. I know his name—it is Martyn."

I referred to Crockford, and presently found "Martyn, Lucian John, Vicar of Slumber-le-Wold, Yorkshire."

"That is the map, I suppose. Was he a personal friend of your husband's?"

"He was a stranger to both of us," she replied, emphatically.

I undertook to obtain a copy of the certificate and wrote the same night to the Rev. Lucian Martyn. To my utter dismay I received in reply a courteous note regretting his inability to comply with my request, as the marriage to which I referred had never been solemnised.

Mr. Martyn's letter reached me by the first post. Two hours later I presented myself at No. 20, Berkeley Square, asked for Miss Ardilaun and was shown into the library. In a few minutes she joined me, and I broke the news as gently as I could.

She seemed utterly overcome. "It is impossible," she repeated; "he cannot deny it. Besides, there are our signatures in the register. Surely he can be made to produce that."

"You are certain that Martyn is the right man?" I asked. "You could swear to his signing the register in that name?"

"No," she replied. "I never saw his signature. I wrote my own name and I saw Arthur write his. Then Parker witnessed our signatures. Mr. Martyn followed, but I did not see what he had written."

"You must excuse my asking questions, Lady Lukestan, where they are necessary. You mentioned that the clergyman who married you was a stranger to both you and your husband. How do you know that he was Mr. Martyn?"

She hesitated.

14

"I knew him from his likeness to his brother."

"You are acquainted with his brother, then?"

"I was. The subject is very painful to me. Mr. Cyprian Martyn is dead. I believe he committed suicide, but our—our friendship had entirely ceased before that took place. I never corresponded with him, and our people were not aware of our acquaintance. It was merely an affair of a few weeks, and terminated very abruptly."

"And the likeness between the brothers was so striking that you recognised Mr. Lucian Martyn immediately."

"The likeness was more than striking, it was—horrible"—she shivered—"if they were both living I should not have known them apart. I was aware that Cyprian Martyn had a brother, who was vicar of a remote parish in Yorkshire, but until the last moment I did not know that he was to marry us. If I had heard the name sooner, I should have used every means in my power to prevent it."

"You are prepared to affirm on oath that your marriage was solemnised by Mr. Martyn in due form, and recorded in the parish register?"

She looked surprised at my question.

"Certainly I am. You surely do not doubt my word?"

"Not at all, but this is a very serious matter. Will you now tell me every detail connected with the ceremony?"

"As I said, I know nothing of the preliminary arrangements. During the third week in January, Lord Lukestan and I were both staying at Chilworth Priory. My aunt was also to have been of the party, but a severe cold detained her in town. Lady Chilworth has great influence with Aunt Maria, and persuaded her to let me go to Yorkshire without her; I was to take part in some theatricals, and my place could not be supplied at the last moment It was the opportunity for which we had been waiting, and we decided not to let it slip. Lord Lukestan's plans were complete. He showed me a special license, and he said Parker knew a village where we could be married, and that all the necessary steps had been taken.

"We left Chilworth on the morning of the 23rd of January. I had previously wired home that the heavy snow would delay my return twenty-four hours. Lady Chilworth was going abroad almost immediately, and as I write all my aunt's letters, I was not afraid of the deception being discovered. We left the train at Garstang, where Parker was waiting with a hired trap, and we drove to this church. There was no one about. The clergyman was waiting for us at the chancel step. He began the service at once. Parker gave me away, and we afterwards signed our names in the vestry. We drove back to the station and caught the next train to Doncaster. I returned to town the following day."

"Was there any conversation between Mr. Martyn and yourselves?"

"None; he did not speak to either of us. Lord Lukestan put the fee on the vestry table. It was a ten-pound note, and he remarked afterwards, that the vicar might have wished us luck. There was no luck for us, I suppose," she concluded bitterly.

I was a good deal puzzled by this sudden check. However, I said what I could to comfort her, and suggested that the clerk could be produced as a witness.

"There was no clerk," she replied, "there was no one in church, but the clergyman, Parker, and ourselves."

From Berkeley Square I hurried to the Temple, found Roskill, and decided with him that I should go up to Slumber-le-Wold, see Martyn, and examine the register.

I found the vicar at home, and acquainted him with my errand. He received me civilly, and in reply to my questions informed me that I was quite at liberty to inspect the register, but it was not possible that I could find any entry of the marriage.

"Since I received your letter," he said, "I have referred to my diary, and I will gladly give you all the information in my power. I find that on the 20th of January I received intimation of an intended wedding. The note, which was brought by a man who looked like a superior servant, had neither address nor date, and was signed Arthur Evelyn Lukestan. I am quite ignorant of the various titles of our aristocracy, and was not aware of the existence of such a person as Lord Lukestan. I was informed the marriage would be by license, and that, owing to certain circumstances, which could be explained to me, if needful, before the ceremony, it was to be of a strictly private character.

"I ascertained that the contracting parties were of age, and fixed the time for one o'clock on the 23rd. Early that morning I was called to the sick bed of a distant parishioner. As I had been advised that the wedding was to be as private as possible, I did not inform the clerk that his services would be required. I intended to do so on my return from Bretwell. Unfortunately, I met with an accident. My horse set its foot on a stone, stumbled, and threw me heavily. I lay for some time unconscious, and when I came to myself, I found my ankle so severely sprained that I was unable to move. The road is a lonely one, and it was at least two hours before I could obtain assistance. I reached home at three o'clock, and immediately sent to the church. There was no one there.

"I afterwards ascertained that a lady and two men, strangers, had passed through the village in the direction of the church, and had returned after the lapse of half an hour. I waited in daily expectation of hearing of or from them, but no news came, and as I did not know Lord, or as I thought, Mr. Lukestan's, address, I was unable to communicate with him. I ought to mention that an open envelope containing a ten-pound note was found on the vestry table. I kept it for three months, anticipating some explanation from the donor, then, as none came, I concluded the money was intended for an offering, and devoted it to the relief of the poor."

I inquired if it were possible that in his absence any other clergyman could have been pressed into the service.

"Quite impossible," he replied. "If any priest could be found willing to commit such a breach of etiquette, he would certainly have informed me of it afterwards; and, in any case, the clerk would have been called."

I said I should like to see the register, and Mr. Martyn led the way to the church.

It stood, as Miss Ardilaun had said, on an eminence at some distance from the village, and was separated from the vicarage by the entire length of the garden and churchyard.

"Is this door always open" I inquired; as we entered the south porch.

"Between *matins* and evensong the church is open for private prayer, though," with a sigh, "my parishioners do not often avail themselves of the privilege."

We went up to the vestry. It was furnished with a table, two chairs, a hanging cupboard, and a massive, iron-bound chest of black oak.

The vicar took a bunch of keys from his pocket, selected one of peculiar shape, unlocked the chest, and produced the register.

"We have not many marriages here," he said. "I have only solemnised two in the last six months. The last was in April."

He turned to the place. There were two entries at the top of the page. The final date on the preceding leaf was for the 30th of December.

I made a minute examination of the pages. Then I glanced keenly at my companion.

"Mr. Martyn," I said, "these two leaves are stuck together."

"Impossible!" he answered.

"Feel them," I rejoined. "This page is thicker than the rest, and the edges are not quite even at the bottom."

He scrutinised the book, testing the substance of the paper between his thumb and forefinger.

"You are quite right," he said, quietly; "though I should never have noticed it. Have you a knife"

I opened my penknife and very carefully inserted the thinnest blade.

How the leaves had been secured, it was impossible to say. There was not the slightest trace of mucilage on the edges of the paper, and the incision once made, they parted easily.

At the top of the left-hand page was the entry of a marriage between Arthur Evelyn Lukestan, bachelor, and Pamela Mary Ardilaun, spinster. The witness was William John Parker.

"My God!"

The exclamation came from the vicar. His eyes were fixed on the register and his face was white to the very lips.

"What is it?" I asked, in surprise.

He pointed speechlessly to the fourth signature. It was written in a firm, very uncommon hand, "Cyprian George Martyn."

"That is not your name, Mr. Martyn?"

He faced me suddenly.

"It is not," he answered. "It is that of my brother Cyprian, who died last October."

I confess I felt horribly taken aback. Miss Ardilaun's admission that she had been acquainted with the younger Martyn taken in connection with the other peculiar circumstances attending her marriage, gave rise in my mind to a most uncomfortable suspicion.

I regarded my client with the sincerest admiration and sympathy. I was anxious to prove the validity of her claims and the truth of her statements, but I could not blind myself to the fact of her position being desperate, and I knew that a desperate woman is frequently unscrupulous.

For a few seconds we remained silent, each, I believe, suspecting the other's complicity in what was evidently a deep-laid plot. Then I pulled myself together.

"You say that is your brother's name, Mr. Martyn, is it also his handwriting?"

"It is like it, very like it, but it can only be a forgery, since, as I told you, my brother is dead."

I examined the entry carefully.

"The particulars are filled in by the same hand, and it would not, I imagine, be an easy one to imitate. Had you seen this signature during your brother's lifetime, should you have had any doubts as to its being genuine?"

"If he were living, none."

"I should like to compare it with an authenticated specimen of his writing, if you have one by you. I need not apologise for the trouble I am giving you, since you will understand that this is, to my client, a matter of life and death, or rather of what is more important than either to a woman, of honour."

"I understand that, and you will have any assistance I can render, but—"

He broke off abruptly, and proceeded to re-lock the chest.

"We will carry the register up to the house. I have some of my brother's letters there, which will serve your purpose."

"Is the register usually kept here?"

"Always."

"And the key, have you more than one? I see it is of a very uncommon pattern."

"So far as I know, there has never been a duplicate."

"And it has not, to your knowledge, left your possession?"

"I am sure it has not. I carry it constantly about my person."

"Had you those keys with you on the 23rd of January?"

"Yes, I am certain of it."

"How, then, was it possible for anyone to get at the register?"

"I cannot tell. It would appear impossible, were it not for that extraordinary entry."

"It would be impossible to tamper with that lock," I said, pointing to the coffer.

"I should have thought so."

We retraced our steps, the vicar carrying the register, which he placed on the table in his study. He then produced a bundle of letters, selected two or three, which he glanced through and handed to me. We compared the signatures with that in the register. They were identical. If a forgery, it was the work of an expert. No amateur could have counterfeited so perfectly those singular characters.

"Your brother's handwriting bears very little resemblance to yours," I remarked. "Were you much alike in person? "

"There was a family likeness, not, I think, very strong; but you can judge for yourself. This is my brother's photograph."

He pointed to a massive silver frame which occupied the centre of the mantel-piece. I went over and studied the portrait. It was a large, three-quarter, platina-type of a tall, handsome man, apparently several years younger than the vicar of Slumber-le-Wold. There was, as he had said, a family likeness between the two faces, but it was not remarkable, and no one could for a moment have mistaken one for the other.

I returned to town, sorely perplexed, drove straight to the Temple, where I had wired, requesting Roskill and, if possible, Miss Ardilaun, to wait for me, and told my story.

Charley was furious. He made some very intemperate and highly absurd charges against the clergy in general, and Mr. Martyn in particular, and declared himself as firmly convinced of Lady Lukestan's good faith as he was of his own.

I ventured to suggest that in this case his convictions were of less moment than those of the judge and jury, and I doubted if any judge would share the opinion he had so confidently expressed. For my part, I could see only three possible solutions of the mystery, (1) That Martyn, who was the only person having access to the register, had, for some private motive, tried to suppress the fact of the marriage, in which case the history of his accident and absence on the 23rd of January was an invention, and could easily be disproved; (2) That Lord Lukestan, finding the vicar absent, had obtained the services either of another clergyman or someone personating the same, and had gone through the marriage ceremony, by way of satisfying Miss Ardilaun's scruples; (3) That the story of the marriage was an entire fabrication, the last resource of a despairing woman, in which case it was impossible to account for the entry in the register.

At this juncture Lady Lukestan was announced. She was dressed in deep, but not widow's, mourning, which became her admirably. She was certainly a very beautiful woman, and, looking into her clear blue eyes, it seemed impossible to doubt her integrity.

I questioned her closely as to her previous statements, but she never swerved a hair's breadth from her original story.

I had brought with me a photograph of Mr. Lucian Martyn, and one of his brother. She looked at the former, and failed to recognise it, though she thought there was something familiar in the expression. I then handed her the portrait of Cyprian Martyn. She gave an involuntary shudder.

"That is the man who married us," she said, and laid the photograph, face downwards, on the table.

"Are you quite sure," I urged, "that you are not making a mistake? The first portrait is that of the present vicar of Slumber-le-Wold, the other that of his brother, who, as you know, is dead."

I shall never forget her expression at that moment, the mingled horror, fear, and repulsion written on her colourless face.

"Then it was he!" she cried. "I knew it. My God! how horrible!"

She made an uncertain step forward, stretching out both hands towards Roskill, with the sudden uncontrollable impulse of blind terror, and slid helplessly to the ground in a dead-faint.

I felt certain then of what I had suspected from the beginning, *viz.*, that Miss Ardilaun knew more of the mystery than she had chosen to confess, and I considered she was treating us unfairly, for a lawyer cannot, any more than a physician, advise on an incomplete diagnosis. She had voluntarily placed herself in our hands, and she ought to have taken us unreservedly into her confidence.

I found an opportunity of expressing these sentiments to Roskill before he escorted her home, and advised him to try to get at the truth. She might speak freely to him. I was sure she had not done so to me.

The more I thought over the bearings of the case, the more I questioned the expediency of taking it into court. The whole weight of evidence told against the plaintiff.

She could not produce a single witness to corroborate his story.

That Lukestan intended to marry her there was no reasonable doubt; but the sole proof of the ceremony having taken place was an entry in the parish register, which was manifestly a forgery.

The only witness whose evidence would have carried any weight, the valet Parker, was dead. It was the bare word of a woman, and a woman in desperate straits, against the reason and common sense of the whole world.

In my opinion, Miss Ardilaun's wisest course would be to keep quiet. Lady Catermaran was now lying in a state of semi-consciousness, and her decease could only be a question of days. Presumably she would have made some provision for her niece, and at her demise Miss Ardilaun would be her own mistress. She might retire somewhere abroad, and her unhappy story need never be given to the world.

But to drag the case into court seemed to be absolutely courting publicity and shame. She might consider herself Lukestan's wife, but, in the eyes of the law and of society, she was simply his mistress, and her child would be declared illegitimate.

And then there remained the question, *had* she really believed herself legally married, or was her story only a last desperate expedient to avert the consequences of a fatal error.

The doubts in Miss Ardilaun's sincerity, which her presence invariably tended to dispel, had an awkward way of returning very forcibly when the magnetism of her personal influence was removed.

Late in the afternoon Roskill returned. I saw at once that he had something to tell me. He threw his hat and gloves on the table, and began to pace restlessly up and down the room.

"It is the most extraordinary case that ever has or will be heard," he said.

"She has told you everything?"

"Yes."

"Did the marriage ever take place, then?"

He looked at me murderously.

"You heard her say so, that ought to be proof enough for you."

It wasn't, but I did not attempt to argue the point. I inquired who had performed the ceremony.

"The man whose name you saw in the register, Cyprian Martyn."

"But he's been dead for the last nine months," I objected. "How could he reappear in the flesh to solemnise a marriage?"

"I don't know," he answered, "how the devil works, or by what laws he is bound. There are some things which cannot be explained. That brute—well, the man is dead, and I won't abuse him, though, living and dead, he's behaved like a brute—got acquainted with Pam—Miss Ardilaun, fell in love with her, and wanted to marry her. She refused him, whereupon he conducted himself in a manner for which his only excuse could be that he was insane at the time. He told her that she had ruined him body and soul, that he meant to have his revenge, and if ever she married, he should marry her, if not himself, then to another man. Then he went back to his parish, somewhere in Dorsetshire, and committed suicide."

"Well," I said, "what has that to do with the Lukestan marriage?"

"Everything—the man kept his word. He did marry her to Lukestan. The poor girl had a secret terror all the time that he had done so, but the thing seemed so incredible that she fought it down and hoped against hope, until it was impossible to doubt any longer."

22

I sat and stared at him blankly. He was absolutely serious.

"Do you really expect me to believe," I said at last, "that a man who has been dead for nine months could rise from his grave, assume bodily form and material clothing, go through a form of prayer, extract a register from a locked chest, make that entry and disappear again into the limbo of the unknown?"

"I don't expect anything. I tell you facts."

"Good heavens, Charley, you must be mad! You can't believe such a monstrous story!"

"I believe it entirely. It is the only rational explanation of that entry."

"*Rational!*" I echoed, contemptuously.

"Yes, rational; for what do we know of the powers and limitations of what we are pleased to call spirits? Nothing. On the other hand, is it reasonable to suppose that three people could obtain access, without a key and without damaging the lock, to a secured chest, abstract the register, the whereabouts of which they were entirely ignorant, and make an entry in the name and handwriting of a dead man—a piece of penmanship, moreover, unrivalled in the annals of forgery? Surely the latter theory is as great a strain on your credulity as the former."

"Take it into court and see what they say to it there?"

"I intend to do so," he answered, quietly.

"No solicitor will undertake the case."

"If you mean that you won't, I shall find someone who will, though I would much rather receive instructions from you than from a stranger."

Then I gave tongue. For two hours I used every argument in my power. I stormed, I persuaded; I believe I threatened, but he remained quite unmoved.

"It isn't the least use, Jack," he said, when at last I stopped, exhausted. "Legally and morally Pamela is Lukestan's widow, and I mean to fight to the last gasp for her rights. If we succeed, so much the better for her and her child. If we fail, well, we shall have done our best to vindicate truth and justice. In either case, I may as well tell you that I intend to make her my wife. Her aunt is not expected to live through the night. She will be alone in the world then, and I shall marry her as soon as I decently can. I believe she has cared for me from the first," he added, softly, with the sublime and overweening credulity of a man who loves.

I doubted it, but what was the use of saying so. Roskill's will has all through our joint lives dominated that of his weaker brother; and when a few days later I heard from Miss Ardilaun's lips the particulars of her extraordinary story, I succumbed to that personal influence which would subdue any man save an incorruptible and unprejudiced judge.

The long and the short of it was that Roskill had his way, and in process of time the case of "Lukestan *v.* Lukestan and others" came on for hearing. Miss Ardilaun's appearance created a profound sensation in court. She told her story simply and directly, and the most severe cross-examination failed to shake her in the smallest detail.

The fact of Lukestan's having taken out a special license, together with his letters (produced), proved he had desired to be, and believed he was, legally married The evidence of the stationmaster at Garstang, of the innkeeper from whom the trap was hired, of the villagers who saw the party pass through Slumber-le-Wold, all confirmed their progress to the very door of the church, but there stretched a gulf which no human witness could bridge.

The personality of the officiating priest, the authorship of the entry in the register, alike remained an inexplicable mystery.

It was admitted on all hands that Roskill's speech was a model of forensic rhetoric. He surpassed the utmost expectations of those who had prophesied for him a brilliant future, and placed himself at once in the front rank of the Junior Bar. But no argument, however powerful, could have convinced a dozen hard-headed, practical Englishmen of the possible existence of ghosts. They were called upon to decide whether Cyprian Martyn, being dead, had resumed his fleshly habit to solemnise a marriage which consigned the woman who had rejected him to shame and obloquy, or whether, on the other hand, Pamela Ardilaun had, with the late Lord Lukestan and Parker, the valet, fraudulently obtained access to the parish register and therein forged the entry of a fictitious marriage—and the twelve good men and true unhesitatingly decided against the ghost.

Judgment was given for the defendant, with costs, and Pamela Ardilaun left the court a ruined woman. The slender fortune left her by her aunt was more than swallowed up by the expenses of the trial. Her fair fame was blasted, she was branded before the world as an impostor and an adventuress. Verily, if her story were true, Cyprian Martyn had taken a complete revenge.

Yet the woman was not left utterly desolate. Through all stress of weather Roskill's love stood firm. He absolutely refused to be dismissed. He assumed the management of her affairs, provided her with a home, and procured the first medical advice when, broken down with anxiety and despair, her life hung trembling in the balance. He followed to the grave the hapless infant, who lived just long enough to receive its father's baptismal names of Arthur Evelyn, and, finally, in spite of her repeated refusals to burden him with her wrecked life, made her his wife.

A year after Lukestan's tragic death the two were married before the registrar. Nothing would have induced either to risk a repetition of the horrors of that other wedding, and as the law takes no cognisance of ghosts, Cyprian Martyn's uneasy spirit was unable to interfere in the civil ceremony which made Miss Ardilaun Charley Roskill's wife.

The Trainer's Ghost

The "Cat and Compass" was shut in for the night. The front of the house was dark and silent, for it was long past closing time, but from one of the rear ground-floor windows a thin shaft of yellow light gleamed through the falling rain, and indicated that behind the shutters of the snug bar-parlour, in a cheerful atmosphere of tobacco smoke and the odorous steam of hot "Scotch" Mr. Samuel Vicary, licensed victualler, and two other congenial spirits, were "making a night of it."

"It's too late for Downey now," the landlord remarked, with a glance at the clock, as he leaned forward to knock out his pipe on the hob. "Twenty past twelve, and raining like blazes. D—— the weather; if it holds on like this, 'The Ghoul' will have his work cut out to get round the old course on Thursday with 8 stone 9."

"Not with that lot behind him," rejoined a seedy individual who sat on the farther side of the table. "I've watched them pretty carefully. The race lies between us and the favourite, and with Downey up, she's safe enough. It's real jam this time—eh, Mr. Davis?"

The gentleman indicated drained his glass with an unctuous smile. His exterior suggested the prosperous undertaker. As a matter of fact, he was a bookmaker in a big way of business, and suspected, moreover, of having considerable interest in a stable notorious for the in and out running of its horses.

"That's about the size of it," he answered, drawing in his thick lips with a gentle, sucking sound, expressive of inward satisfaction.

"Prime whisky this, Vicary! I'll take another tot. Yes, it is a big thing, and, after this, Davis, Smiles, and Co. must lie quiet for a bit. There'll be plenty of fools to cry over burnt fingers by Monday, and what with stewards meddling where they've no cause to interfere, and the press writing up a lot of rot about 'rings' and such like, and the Jockey Club holding inquiries, a man must mind his P's and Q's in these days. Racing is going to the dogs, and soon there'll be no making a decent living on the turf. How it does rain to be sure! I shouldn't care to find myself abroad tonight."

"Here's some poor devil as has got to face it," said the tout, as the sound of horse-hoofs echoed down the quiet road. "Ain't he coming a lick, too! He's not afraid of bustling his cattle."

"Small blame to him either in weather like this," grunted the landlord, removing his pipe to listen. "Why, that's Downey's hack. I'd swear to her gallop among a thousand. To think, now, of his turning up at this time of night!"

The clatter of hoofs ceased, and the men sprang to their feet. In the silence that followed they heard the muffled slam of a closing gate, and the clink of shoes on the stones of the yard outside. Vicary snatched up the lamp and hurried to the door, while the visitors looked at each other.

"'Tis Downey sure enough," said the bookmaker, spitting energetically into the fire. "Now, what brings him here so late? He hasn't pelted over from Hawkhurst in the teeth of this storm for the pleasure of our company, I'll go bail."

The newcomer had swung himself off his horse before the landlord could unfasten the door.

"Yes, it's me—Downey," was his answer to that worthy's cautious challenge. "Look sharp with that chain and let me get under cover. I'm stiff with the cold, I can tell you, and the mare is about beat."

The chain fell with a clank, and Vicary flung back the door.

"Come in, come in," he cried, holding the lamp above his head to get a better view of his visitor.

"Lord! how it do rain! Get out of that coat and put a tot of whisky inside you, while I see to the mare. 'Tis all right," he added, as the other jerked his head interrogatively in the direction of the bar-parlour, "there's only me and Slimmy and Davis. Go right in and help yourself."

Thus assured, the fresh arrival went forward, the water dripping from his soaked hat and covert coat, and trickling in little black streams over the well-stoned passage; while Vicary, flinging a rug across his shoulders, led the tired horse round to the stables.

When he returned to the parlour Downey was drying himself before the fire, a smoking tumbler in his hand, and a good cigar between his lips.

"Well?" inquired the landlord, setting down the lamp with a keen glance at the disturbed countenances of the three men. "I take it, you did not come through this rain for nothing. Is aught the matter?"

"Matter enough," ejaculated Slimmy. "Here's Coulson got a rod in pickle that is going to upset our pot."

Vicary laughed.

"Go on with you," he said derisively, "they've nothing at Malton as can collar the Ghoul."

"Don't you be so precious sharp," the tout retorted. "Wait till you hear what Downey's got to say."

The jockey shifted his cigar to the other side of his mouth. "It is this way," he began. "One of Coulson's lads was at our place this afternoon, and he let on to me in confidence that they have a colt over there they think a real good thing for the Ebor. It is entered in Berkeley's name—the Captain, him as sold the Malton place to Coulson."

"The Captain's been stony broke this three year," put in Vicary. "How did he come by the colt?"

"Picked him up in the dales, from what I gather (he'd always a rare eye for a horse had the Captain), and fancied him so that he got young Alick to take half-share, and lend the purchase-money into the bargain, I reckon. The Coulsons always thought a lot of the old family. It wouldn't be the first time one of them had helped a Berkeley out of a tight place."

"That's true," assented the landlord. "Markham told me old Alick held enough of the squire's paper to cover a room. There wasn't anything he'd have stuck at to keep him on his legs. I remember him saying once in that very bar there, 'I'd come from hell,' he says, 'to stand by one of the old stock.' Fifteen years ago this very day it was, just before the Ebor, and the last time I ever saw the old chap alive, for Blue Ruin kicked the life out of him in his box at Malton on the morning of the race. Nothing would serve the squire but the horse must be shot the same night. Lord, what a shindy there was! And if it weren't like one of old Berkeley's fool's-tricks to 'blue' twelve hundred pounds that way, and him not knowing where to turn for the ready! But about this colt: if he's such a clipper, how is it nobody's heard of him before this?"

"Coulson has kept him dark. He's been trained at Beverley, and they only brought him to Malton three weeks back. The lad tells me he has been doing very good work, and he is to be tried in the morning with Cream Cheese—that is schoolmaster to the Leger crack. Now look here, if the colt can beat Cream Cheese at a stone, he's a moral for the Ebor. On a heavy course he'll walk right away from the Ghoul, and put us in the cart."

The landlord whistled.

"You are sure the lad's square?"

"I'd peel the flesh off his bones if I thought he was putting the double on me; but he daren't try it. Coulson as good as swore the boys over to hold their tongues, but Tom says the stable is that sweet on his chance, they'll put their shirts on the colt at starting-price."

"Who's to ride him?"

"Alick's head lad. The brute has a temper, and won't stand much "footling" about; but Jevons and he understand each other, and his orders are to get him off well, and sit still."

"I suppose now," suggested the bookmaker, "this Jevons ain't a reasonable sort of chap?"

Downey grinned. "As well try to square Coulson himself. He is one of your Sunday-school-and-ten-commandments sort, is Jevons. Besides, his father was the old squire's second horseman, and the lad was brought up in the stables. He swears by the Berkeleys, and would never lend a hand to put a spoke in the captain's wheel."

"Do you know what time the trial is to come off?"

"About six. I reckoned on Slimmy's being within call, for there is precious little time to lose. It is light by four."

"I'm game," said the tout, "if Mr. Vicary will lend me something to take me over."

The landlord consulted his watch. "Half-past one," he said. "Let's see; it's close on fifteen mile to Coulson's. I'll drop you at the Pig and Whistle. You can get over the fields from Gunny's corner in twenty minutes."

"You know your way?" queried Davis, uneasily.

"Every yard of it, guv'nor. Coulson and me is old friends so long as we don't happen to meet. There is a nice bit of cover at the end of the ground where I can lie snug. Will you wait for me, Mr. Vicary?"

"Aye, I'll be on the road by Gunny's at seven. What for you, Downey; can we give you a shakedown here?"

"No thank you; I'm off," answered the jockey, laughing; "you're altogether too warm in this corner for a nice young man like me. I'm putting up at the Great Northern, and shall see you and Davis for the first time on the course, and not more than I can help of you then."

The rain had cleared off, and the first pale rifts in the eastern sky were broadening into grey dawn before Mr. Slimmy, from the convenient elevation of a friendly elder bush, caught sight of a line of dark specks moving across the wold, and gradually resolving themselves into a string of horses.

"Here they come," he murmured, pocketing the flat bottle from which he had been refreshing his inner man, and working himself cautiously forward on the stout bough, while he parted the leaves with his left hand to command a better view. "And here's young Alick and the Captain. I thought as much," he added, triumphantly, for the trainer and Berkeley had cantered up and reined in their hacks within ten paces of his hiding-place.

In a very few minutes the horses were stripped and got into line.

"They will start themselves," said Coulson, "and take it easy for the first half mile. Then you'll see, Captain, that there is very little fear but what the colt will give a good account of himself tomorrow. There they go, and a good start too."

The horses jumped off together, a big chestnut, which even in the half-light Slimmy had recognised as Cream Cheese, coming to the front, with a clear lead. The soft drum of the hoofs on the moist ground died away, and the two men stood up in their stirrups, following with keen eyes the dim outline of the horses as they rounded the curve and swept into the straight, the chestnut still showing the way, with his stable companion and a powerful-looking bay in close attendance. "There he goes!" was the tout's mental ejaculation, for, at the bend for home, a dark horse crept up on the inside, and, taking up the running at half distance, came on and finished easily with a couple of lengths to spare.

Coulson turned to his companion with a smile.

"He'll do, Captain. The money is as good as banked. You can put on his clothes, Jevons, and take him home. He's a clipper, and no mistake. He came up the straight like a—"

"Rocket," suggested Berkeley. "How's that for a name? By Gunpowder out of Falling Star—not bad, I think."

"Couldn't be better," was the hearty answer.

"A few more of his sort, and we'll soon have you back at the Hall, Master Charles. I shall live to lead in a Derby winner for you yet. Lord! I think it would almost bring the old man out of his grave to know the Berkeley's had their own again."

The words were hardly past his lips when a crack, like the report of a pistol, close behind them, made both men jump as if they had been shot.

31

Mr. Slimmy, who, having heard and seen all he wanted, was in the act of beating a masterly retreat, had unfortunately set his foot on a rotten branch, which instantly snapped beneath his weight. Taken by surprise, the tout lost his foothold and his balance at the same time, made an ineffectual grab at the swinging boughs, pitched forward, and, despite his wild endeavours to recover himself, descended precipitately in a shower of leaves and dry twigs on the wrong side of the hedge.

"Where the deuce did the fellow come from?" ejaculated Berkeley, as he gazed blankly at the heap on the ground. Coulson's only answer was to swing himself off his horse and fling the bridle to his companion.

The quick-witted trainer had reckoned up the situation in a moment, and before the luckless Slimmy could gather himself together Coulson's hand was on his collar, and Coulson's "crop" was cracking and curling about his person, picking out the tenderest parts with a scientific precision that made him writhe and twist in frantic efforts to free himself from that iron grip. But the trainer stood six feet in his socks, and was well built. He held his victim like a rat, while his strong right arm brought the lash whistling down again and again with a force that cut through the tout's seedy clothing like a knife.

"For God's sake, Coulson," cried Captain Berkeley, "hold hard, or you will kill the man."

"And a good thing, too," said the trainer, relinquishing his hold on Slimmy with a suddenness that sent him sprawling into the muddy ditch. "I know him, and I'll have no touting on my place. If he shows his face here again, he'll find himself in the horse-pond. Stop that row," he went on, turning to where Slimmy lay in the ditch, crying and cursing alternately; "and get off my ground before I chuck you over the fence."

White with rage and pain, the tout picked himself up and scrambled through the gap in the hedge as fast as his aching limbs could carry him. But when he had put a safe distance between himself and Coulson, he turned and shook his fist at the trainer's retreating figure.

"Curse you," he said, with a horrible imprecation. "I'll pay you out for this. I'll be even with you, if I swing for it, swelp me if I ain't."

Owner and trainer rode home in silence.

Coulson was a good deal upset by the discovery that his horse was being watched. He had recognised Slimmy, and Slimmy was known to be in the employ of a party popularly supposed to stick at nothing, and quite capable of trying to get at a horse that threatened to upset their game. Then, again, the arrangements and time of the trial had been kept so quiet that it seemed impossible the tout could get wind of it, except from some, one directly connected with the stables. Altogether Coulson felt uneasy, and, after some consideration, he mentioned his suspicions to his head lad, in whom he had the most implicit confidence. Jevons thought things over for a bit. Then he suggested the colt's box should be changed, and that he should sit up with him.

"Put him in the end box next the saddle-room, sir; it is so seldom used that an outsider would not think of trying it, and there isn't many of the lads as would like to rux about in there tonight, leastways not one as has a bad conscience."

Coulson knew what he meant. In the box next the saddle-room his father, old Alick Coulson, had come by his end, kicked to death by the Ebor favourite on the very eve of the race. A training-stable is not exactly a hot-bed of superstition, but, without doubt, a feeling did exist in connection with that particular box, and, as Jevons had said, it was very rarely used.

"Shall you like to sit up there yourself?" the trainer asked bluntly.

Jevons did not mind at all. He said he did not hold with ghosts and such like, and he was sure a sportsman like the old master would know better than to come upsetting the colt and spoiling his, Jevons's, nerve just before the race. Still, as there was gas in the saddle-room and a fire, if Mr. Coulson had no objection, he might as well sit there, and look in every now and again to see his charge next door was getting on all right.

The trainer readily agreed. He had a high opinion of the lad's coolness and common sense, but he also felt that to pass the night alone and without a light in a place which, however undeservedly, had the reputation of being haunted, and that, too, on the very anniversary of the tragedy from which the superstition took its rise, was a performance calculated to try the strongest nerves, and he preferred that Jevons should not face the ordeal.

Indeed, it struck him as he left the lad for the night that he would scarcely have cared to undertake the watch himself. It might be fancy, but there was a queer feel about the place.

"Fifteen years ago tonight," thought Coulson, "since an Ebor crack stood in that box. It was a dark horse, too, and owned by the squire. It is a coincidence, anyway. No, I shouldn't care to take on Jevons's job."

Nor was he alone in his conclusions. Several other people expressed a similar conviction, notably Jevons's subordinate, who had heard of the arrangement in the morning.

"I wouldn't be in Bill's shoes tonight—no, not for fifty down," he said, and slipped off unobserved to the nearest box to post a letter.

The communication he despatched was addressed to "S. Downey, Esq., Great Northern Hotel, York," and was marked "immediate." The lad was going over to the races in the afternoon, and felt tolerably certain of getting speech with the jockey; but he was a careful young man, and wisely left nothing to chance.

****

It wanted fifteen minutes to midnight. Outside, the night was as black as your hat: not a vestige of a moon, not a single star to break the uniform darkness of the sky. With sunset a noisy blustering wind had sprung up, rattling about the chimneys, clashing the wet branches, and deadening the sound of cautious footfalls creeping across the paddock in the direction of the stables. Jevons was sitting over the saddle-room fire, with his pipe and the *Sporting Life* for company, and the remains of his supper-beer on the table beside him. From time to time he took a lantern and went to look at his charge. The colt had been quiet enough all the earlier part of the evening, but for the last half-hour Jevons fancied he could hear him fidgeting about on the other side of the wall.

"What ails the brute?" he said to himself, laying down his pipe to listen.

The wind dropped suddenly, making the silence all the more intense by contrast with the previous roar; and through the stillness Jevons heard the clink of a bucket, and the sound of someone moving about in the loose-box.

He sprang to his feet and snatched up the lantern. His sole idea was that someone was trying to get at the horse, and his hand was on the revolver in his breast-pocket when he opened the door. So strong was the impression that he was positively surprised to find no sign of an intruder. The colt was lying in the farthest corner and perfectly quiet. Jevons looked all round. There was certainly nothing to see, but it struck him that the air felt very cold, and he shut the door. The instant it closed behind him, a dark shadow fell across the square of light issuing from the entrance to the saddle-room.

"Now's your time, Slimmy," whispered Mr. Vicary. "Nip in and doctor his liquor. This is getting precious slow."

The beer stood on a table barely two paces from the door. Stretching out his arm, the tout emptied the contents of a small bottle into the jug, and crept noiselessly back to his hiding-place.

"There's a deuce of a draught in here," said Jevons to himself, "and where it comes from fairly beats me."

He held up his hand at different heights, trying to test the direction of the chill current of air. But it seemed to come from every quarter at once, and shifted continually.

The lad struck a lucifer, and held it level with his shoulder. To his utter astonishment the flame burned clear and steady, though he could feel the cold draught blowing on his face, and even stirring the hair on his closely cropped head.

"That's a rum go," he said, staring at the match as it died out. He backed a few steps towards the wall, the draught was fainter; when he came level with the horse it ceased altogether.

"You are wise, my lad, to stick to this corner," Jevons remarked as he looked at the colt; "it's enough to blow your head off on the other side. Well, it must have been the wind I heard, for there ain't nothing here."

He locked the door and went back to the saddle-room. The hands of the American clock on the narrow mantelpiece pointed to twelve. Jevons loaded his pipe, poured out the rest of the beer, and took a long pull. Then he kicked the fire together, and looked about for a match.

"Now, where did I put that box," he said, staring stupidly round. "Where did I put that—what is it I'm looking for? What's got my head? It's all of a swim."

He felt for a chair and sat down, holding his hand to his heavy eyes. The lids felt as if they were weighted with lead. The gas danced in a golden mist that blinded him, and the whole room was spinning round and round. Then the pipe dropped from his nerveless lingers, and his head forward on the table.

"He's safe," muttered Vicary, as he softly pushed the door ajar and surveyed the unconscious lad. "That's prime stuff to keep the baby quiet. Here's the key, Slimmy; I'll bring the light. When we've damped the powder in that there Rocket, Coulson will wish he hadn't been so handy with his crop this morning."

Slimmy turned the key in the lock and looked into the box; then he gave a slight start, and drew quickly back.

"What's up?" inquired the landlord. "Go on, it's all right."

"Sh!" whispered the tout, "he might hear you."

"Hear us? not he, nor the last day neither, if it come now."

He was thinking of Jevons, but Slimmy pulled to the door and held it.

"There's someone in there," he muttered, "an old chap. He's sitting on a bucket right in front of the horse."

"Did he see you?"

"I don't know, his back was turned and he looked asleep like."

He leaned forward, listening intently, but not a sound came from behind the closed door.

"Coulson didn't mean to be caught napping," said Vicary, under his breath. "Is it a stable hand?"

"A cut above that," returned the other, in the same tone. "'Tis queer he should keep so quiet."

They waited a few minutes, but everything was still.

"See here," whispered Slimmy, untwisting the muffler he wore round his neck, "there ain't no manner of use standing here all night Give me the stick. If I can get past him quiet, I will; but if he moves, you be ready to slip the handkerchief over his head. He can't make much of a fight agen the two of us, and we ain't got this far to be stalled off by an old crock like him; keep well behind him. Never mind the lantern. He's got a light inside."

There was a light inside, but where it came from would have been difficult to say. It fell clear as a limelight over half the box, and beyond the shadow lay black and impenetrable, a wall of darkness.

As he crossed the threshold Slimmy felt a blast of cold air sweep towards him, striking a strange chill into his very bones.

Straight opposite stood a horse, and before him an old man was sitting on a reversed bucket, his elbow resting on his knee, his head on his hand. To all appearances he was asleep. But even in that intense stillness the tout could catch no sound of breathing. His own heart was thumping against his ribs with the force of a sledge-hammer. He felt his flesh creeping with a sensation of fear that was almost sickening. Fear? Yes, that was the word; he was horribly afraid. And of what? Of a weak old man, for whom he would have been more than a match single-handed, and they were two to one. What a fool he was, to be sure!

With a desperate effort he pulled himself together and went forward, his eye warily fixed on the silent figure. Neither man nor horse moved. Slimmy thrust his hand into his pocket and felt for the bottle which was to settle the Rocket's chances for the Ebor! His fingers were on the cork, when the silence was broken by a sound that brought a cold sweat out on his forehead and lifted the hair on his head. It was a low chuckling laugh. The man on the bucket was looking at him. The gleaming eyes fixed him with a sort of mesmeric power, and the bottle fell from his trembling fingers.

"Quick with the rag, Sam," he gasped, "he's seen me." But Vicary stood like one turned to stone. His gaze fastened on the seated figure, taking in every item of the quaint dress, the high gill collar and ample bird's-eye stock, the drab coat and antiquated breeches and gaiters. His mouth was open, but for the life of him he could not speak. He was waiting in the helpless fascination of horror to see the face of a man who had been dead and buried for fifteen years.

Slowly, like an automaton, that strange watcher turned his head. The square, resolute mouth was open as if to speak; the shrunken skin was a greenish yellow colour, like the skin of a corpse; along the temple ran a dull blue mark in the shape of a horse's hoof; but the eyes burned like two living coals, as they fixed themselves on the face of the terrified publican.

With a single yell of "Lord ha' mercy on us! 'tis old Alick himself!" Vicary turned and fled.

Slimmy heard the crash of the lantern on the stones and the sound of his flying feet, and an awful terror came upon him, a great fear, which made his teeth chatter in his head and curdled the blood in his veins.

The place seemed full of an unnatural light—the blue flames that dance at night over deserted graveyards. The air was foul with the horrible odours of decay. Above all, he felt the fearful presence of that which was neither living nor dead—the semblance of a man whose human body had for fifteen years been rotting in the grave. It was not living, but it moved. Its cold, shining eyes were looking into his, were coming nearer. Now they were close to him. With the energy of despair, Slimmy grasped his stick by the thin end and struck with his full force at the horror before him. The loaded knob whistled through empty air, and, overbalanced by the force of his own blow, the wretched tout pitched forward, and with one piercing shriek fell prone on the straw.

★★★★★★★★

"Did you hear that?"

"What the deuce was it?"

The two men, who were sitting over the fire in the comfortable

37

smoking-room, sprang to their feet. Coulson put down his pipe and went into the hall. Someone was moving about in the kitchen.

"Is that you, Martin?" he called. "What was that row?"

The man came out at once.

"Did you hear it too, sir? It made me jump, it came so sudden. Sounded like someone hollering out in the stables."

"Get a lantern. I must go across and see what it was. Are you coming, too, Captain? Then bring that shillelagh in your hand. It might be useful."

Martin unbolted the side door, which opened on the garden, and the three men crossed the gravel path and went through the yard. Here they saw the gleam of another lantern. Someone was running towards them. It was one of the lads, half dressed, and evidently just out of bed.

"Is that you, Mr. Coulson?" he said breathlessly. "Did you hear that scream? It woke us all up. Bryant can see the saddle-room from his window, and he says the door is wide open."

"Come on," was Coulson's answer, as they hurried across to the stables. The square of light from the saddle-room showed clearly through the darkness.

"Here's Jevons," said the trainer, who was the first to enter. "He is only asleep," he added, as he lifted the lad's head and listened to the regular breathing. He shook him roughly, trying to arouse him, but Jevons was beyond being awakened by any ordinary method; he made an inarticulate grunt, and dropped back into his former attitude.

"Drunk?" ejaculated Martin, blankly.

"Drugged, by gad!" Captain Berkeley had taken the empty jug from the table and smelt it The sickly odour of the powerful opiate clung about the pitcher and told its own tale.

"Then," cried the trainer, "as I'm a living man, they've got at the colt." His face was white and set as he seized the lantern and ran to the loose-box. The door was open; the key was in the lock. The men crowded up. There was scarcely a doubt in their minds but that the mischief was already done. Coulson held up the lantern and looked round. The colt was standing up in the corner, snorting and sniffing the air. He, too, had been startled by that terrible cry.

On the ground, straight in front of the door, a man lay prone on his face. There was no mistaking the look of that helpless body, the limp flaccidity of those outstretched arms.

"He's dead, sir," said Martin, as he turned up the white face; "hold the light down; his coat's all wet with—something."

It was not blood, only a sticky, dark-coloured fluid, the contents of a broken bottle lying underneath the body. Just beyond the reach of the clenched right hand was a heavy loaded-stick, and near the door they found a thick woollen handkerchief. Berkeley bent down and looked at the drawn features.

"Surely," he said, in a low voice, "it is the same man you thrashed this morning?"

Coulson nodded. "He meant squaring accounts with me, and he has had to settle his own instead. It is strange that there should be no marks of violence about him, and yet he looks as if he had died hard."

And truly, the dead man's face was terrible in its fixed expression of mortal fear. The eyes were staring and wide open, the teeth clenched, a little froth hung about the blue lips. It was a horrid sight. They satisfied themselves that life was absolutely extinct. Then Coulson gave orders for the colt to be taken back to his old box, locked the door on the corpse until the police could arrive, and spent the remainder of the night in the saddle-room, waiting till Jevons should have slept off the effects of the opiate.

But when the lad awoke, he could throw very little light on the matter. He swore positively there was no one in the box when he paid his last visit at five minutes to twelve, and he could remember nothing after returning to the saddle-room. How the tout had effected an entrance, by what means his purpose had been frustrated and his life destroyed, remained for ever a mystery. The only living man who knew the truth held his tongue, and the dead can tell no tales. But Mr. Vicary, as he watched Captain Berkeley's colt walk away from his field next day, and, cleverly avoiding a collision with the favourite on the rails, pass the post a winner by three lengths, was struck by the fact that the "Rocket" had grown smaller during the night, and he could have sworn the horse he saw in the loose-box had some white about him somewhere.

"He's one o' raight sort," exclaimed a stalwart Yorkshireman who stood at Vicary's elbow. "When aa seed him i't' paddock, aa said aa'l hev a poond on th' squoire's 'oss for t' saake of ould toimes, for he's strange and loike Blue Ruin, as won th' Ebor in seventy- foive. 'Twas fust race as iver aa'd clapped eyes on, and aa'd backed him for ivery penny aa'd got."

The publican turned involuntarily to the speaker. "Did you say yon colt was like Blue Ruin?" he asked hoarsely.

"The very moral of him, barring he ain't quite so thick, and ain't got no white stocking. I reckon you'll remember Blue Ruin," added the farmer, referring to a friend on the other side, "him as killed ould Coulson?"

Vicary was a strong man, but at the mention of that name a strange, sickly sensation crept over him. The colour forsook his face, and when, a few minutes later he called for a brandy "straight," the hand he stretched out for the glass was shaking visibly.

Once, and once only, did the landlord allude to the events of that fatal night. It was when Mr. Davis, loudly deploring his losses, expressed an opinion that Slimmy was "a clumsy fool, and matters would have come out very differently if he had been there."

"You may thank your stars," was Vicary's energetic rejoinder, "that you never set foot in the cursed place. The poor chap is dead, and there ain't no call for me to get myself mixed up in the business. Least said, soonest mended, say I; but you mind the story I told you the night Downey brought the news of that blooming colt, about ould Coulson swearing he'd come back from the dead, if need be, to do a Berkeley a good turn."

"I remember right enough. What's that got to do with it?"

The landlord glanced nervously over his shoulder. "Only this," he answered, sinking his voice to a whisper: *"he kept his word!"*

The Ghost in the Chair

This story requires explanation. The explanation will never be given, because no one of the theories of cerebral pressure, spectral illusion, or hypnotic influence, by which people try to explain away the inexplicable, can get rid of the single fact that, shortly after three o'clock on a certain Friday afternoon, one hundred and fifty sane and sober men saw, or thought they saw, Curtis Yorke take the chair at a general meeting of the San Sacrada Mining Company, Limited, at which time, according to subsequent medical evidence, he must have been dead for several hours.

For some time, his friends had known that Yorke was going a little bit too fast. While hardly more than a boy, one brilliant hit had gained him a reputation in the City far beyond his years, and at an age when most men are expending their superfluous energy on the tennis-court or river, he was finding brains for the working out of several big undertakings.

Six years of unbroken success taught him to believe his luck infallible. When that changed, as sooner or later it was bound to do, he began to lose confidence in himself. Like many men, who keep a level head in prosperity, he could not play a losing game, and for months past anxiety and overwork had been telling steadily on his nerves.

Moreover, he was superstitious, and though he made no profession of religion, he retained an odd belief in the Puritanical dogmas of hell-fire and a personal devil. This in some measure accounts for what he said to Fielden four days before his tragic end.

The directorate of the San Sacrada Mining Company had been holding an extraordinary meeting. A crisis was impending, and things looked black for the company, which was no "bubble speculation," but a sound and solid concern, suffering from the effects of a persistent run of bad luck.

Now, luck has more to do with the making or marring of mines and men than the moralists would have us believe, and the luck of the San Sacrada Mining Company had all along been execrable.

Unexpected hitches had occurred in securing the title to the property. The contractors had seen fit to export the machinery reversely to the order in which it was required. Delays had been caused by scarcity of water, and when at last the returns promised to justify the small fortune sunk in the shaft, the Yankee manager, whose appointment had been backed by flaming testimonials, demonstrated his native 'cuteness by "skipping out" with twenty-five thousand dollars of the company's money. His place was filled by an Englishman in every way qualified for the post; but before the good effects of this change of administration could become apparent the mine was flooded, and all operations for the time being perforce suspended. Nor was this all.

Unpleasant rumours began to circulate as to the stability of the concern. It was said that money had been borrowed at a ruinous rate of interest; that the company was insolvent; that the very plant had already been seized by their creditors.

One of the financial journals got hold of the story, and treated it after its own inimitable fashion. The company brought an action against the paper, and won their case, thereby incurring heavy law expenses and advertising the scandal, for the public to a man read the offending article, while only a very small section took the trouble to acquaint themselves with the proofs of its inaccuracy.

The shareholders grew restive, and it became known that the forthcoming general meeting was likely to be stormy. It was then that the Board held their extraordinary council. There was much discussion, and many futile suggestions, but no resolution was passed, because, if the situation were to be saved, it would be the work of one man, and he hadn't had time to think out a plan of action. This was the chairman, Curtis Yorke, who, having nothing to say, had said it exceedingly well, and was now aimlessly scribbling on the back of some papers lying before him on the table.

The boardroom was almost deserted. Four of the five directors had gone home; the fifth remained at the special request of the chairman, who had then relapsed into silence and hieroglyphs.

A casual observer might have judged his occupation mere idling, and interrupted him without hesitation. Fielden knew better.

He not unfrequently annoyed his own clients during important interviews by adorning his blotting-pad with minutely detailed presentments of cutters and yawls, and he understood that miscellaneous sketching may be on occasion the outcome of deep thought.

Therefore, he waited, leisurely drawing on his gloves, until at the end of twenty minutes Yorke, without lifting his head from the paper, began to speak.

He said in a low, even voice that the company was going to the devil; that there was only one man who might be induced to see them through, and he was on the Continent, and his exact address uncertain.

That the most important thing now was to gain time, and for that purpose they must find a smart junior, a man who could talk and wasn't too well known; give him five shares and a cheque for fifty guineas, and put him on at the general meeting to impress the shareholders with the necessity for keeping quiet.

He went on to say that the San Sacrada Mine was the third venture that had gone wrong within six months, and that he, Yorke, regarded it as an omen. That if it came to grief, he should never do another stroke of business; that he would be down and done for.

But that it should *not* come to grief, because he intended to pull it through at the price of his own soul. That he was prepared to sell his soul for that end, and he believed the sale would shortly be concluded.

At that moment the fire crackled, and Yorke jumped as if he had been shot. Then he laughed rather awkwardly, and explained that he had not slept for a fortnight, and his nerves were all to pieces.

"I believe," he said apologetically, "that I've been talking d—— rot. To tell the truth, I don't know all the time what I'm saying. It's this beastly insomnia. But you understand what I want for Friday, I made that clear. We must have someone to tackle this Simpson brute, or he'll carry the whole meeting with him. Nothing the Board can say will weigh with the shareholders; but a split among themselves may gain time, and time is money to us just now."

Fielden thought he knew a man who would do, and he asked who Simpson was.

"A dirty little outside broker. The miserable beast hasn't more than a hundred shares in all; but he's quite capable of upsetting our cart as things are at present."

"It is always the small holders who give the most trouble," said Fielden, preparing to go. "I'll see my man tonight, and send you a wire in the morning. If I were you, Yorke, I'd look in at my doctor's on the way home, and get him to give me some bromide or something. You're running under too big a strain. It isn't nice to hear a sensible man talking nonsense about his soul. If you came out with that sort of thing at a meeting the reporters would say you were drunk. Besides, there's no demand for the article nowadays. They are altogether too cheap. Goodnight."

Yorke went with him to the door.

It was raining hard, and the evening air felt raw and chilly. He shivered as he returned to the empty boardroom. His head felt heavy, and there were two pink spots on the green cloth which worried him.

He sat down again at the table and began to play with his pen, writing odd words on the blank sheet of paper.

He certainly had been a fool to let himself go in that way before Fielden. He must have been a bit off his head. And yet it was true. He would sell his soul if that would ensure his coming safely through this business.

His soul! Fielden had said souls were cheap. If City men had souls, what mean, shabby things some of them would be. Yorke tried to imagine what one would look like and laughed. His laugh was not good to hear.

And yet it was a big price to offer, for it was the last possession of the human being—the only thing he has to carry out of this world into the blank Beyond. And it could burn!

He remembered a picture he had seen as a child in an old Bible, of souls burning in hell. Souls with human faces horribly distorted by pain. Yes, that was the end of lost souls—hot fire.

The rain swirled against the long windows, and Yorke's teeth chattered. He was cold now, and the company was going to smash. He had said all along, if this venture went down, he should go with it. It had come to mean everything or nothing to him, and to know for certain that he was going to pull it through he *would* sell his soul.

He began writing again, the words forming themselves automatically beneath his fingers—

I, the undersigned, hereby covenant and agree to guarantee the loan of such moneys as shall cover the working expenses of the San Sacrada Gold Mine for the space of six calendar months, and further to insure the complete success of the company, in consideration of the surrender of the soul of Curtis Yorke, chairman, at such time and for such purpose as I may hereafter determine.

(Signed) x his mark.

It was the merest vagary of a disordered brain, but Yorke's heart gave a great bound as he read and re-read the words.

Then his jaw fell, and his face grew set and rigid with terror, the terror that wipes out all manly strength and courage, and leaves room for nothing but an abject, shaking cowardice. The perspiration stood out in great drops on his forehead, and his eyes were bolting out of his head as he gazed at the paper before him.

On the blank space left for the signature for letters had come out in characters that shimmered and glowed as if they were traced in flame.

Every drop of blood in Yorke's body went to his heart. For one awful moment he remained paralysed and immovable. The next, with a desperate effort, he had seized the sheet of foolscap, and, staggering across the room, flung it into the fire.

The thick paper shrivelled, curled, and broke into a blaze. Yorke snatched up the poker and stirred the coals to a fiercer heat, crushing the charred fragments into the glowing embers.

Then the poker fell from his hand with a crash, and he sank into the nearest chair, shaking and sweating like a scared pony.

The clock on the mantlepiece struck six, and the sound recalled him to a sense of mundane things. He stood up and passed his hand across his damp forehead.

"Good God!" he muttered, "my head must be going. It wasn't real. It couldn't be real. Fielden's right. I'm running under too big a strain. I'll see Jones at once, and get something to pull me together."

He put on his overcoat and went downstairs.

A clerk was coming up the passage with a telegram in his hand.

Yorke stopped under the gas-burner to open the yellow envelope, and his face turned a shade paler as he read the contents.

It was the message for which he had been waiting all day. The address of the one man who could save the company.

This happened on Monday. By Wednesday afternoon Yorke had reached Paris, seen Van Hooten, and brought their conference to a successful issue.

His conduct of the transaction was throughout masterly, and aroused the great financier to an almost paternal expression of admiration.

"You are von ver' clever, young man," he said to Yorke at the close of the interview. "I haf watched you for three, four, five years, and I say to myself, 'He does go far, zat boy; but he will arrive.' What! you made von leetle mistake last Spring about those 'Guatemalas.' Zat is nothing. I myself haf also made mistakes. You are young; you buy your experience. So! But, in ze end, you will succeed, for you haf a head. *Mein Gott!* What a head for a man so young. You see, I haf belief in you. I lend you my influence. I trust you with my money, because I look for you one day to do great things. There is no fear. You will succeed."

"I shall succeed this time," said Yorke.

He took leave of the big man gratefully, for Van Hooten had been a good friend to him.

When he got back to his hotel, he locked himself into his room and drew a paper out of his pocketbook. It was an exact duplicate of the weird bond he had burned in the boardroom on the Monday evening. Impelled by an insane desire to see if the horrible delusion would repeat itself, he had three times re-written the document, watching with a painful admixture of interest and dismay the ghastly signature come out on the white paper. Then, in an access of terror, he would destroy the evidence of his unholy compact, only to reproduce it on the first occasion he found himself alone.

Meanwhile, the treatment prescribed by his doctor exercised a slightly beneficial effect. He did not sleep, but his brain, on the single point in which he was vitally interested, became phenomenally clear, and his powers of endurance appeared to be practically unlimited.

In the three days intervening between the board and general meetings Yorke did the work of ten men. On the Thursday night he devoted himself to the preparation of his speech. He told his servant, who left him in his own room at eleven o'clock, to put a glass of milk and a syphon of soda beside the bed, and on no account to disturb him in the morning until he rang for his shaving-water.

He was then writing. The man went to bed. Yorke must have worked late into the night, for he had made a fair copy of the rough draft of his speech and added several sheets of notes.

When the speech was delivered, it was noticed that, contrary to custom, the chairman used no notes at all. He brought with him no papers whatever, and he arrived very late.

The room was packed, and the general temper of the meeting so manifestly turbulent that Fielden's neighbour had given it as his opinion that if Yorke did not turn up soon, neither he nor anyone else would be able to obtain a hearing.

The words were scarcely past his lips before the tall figure of the chairman became visible amidst the crowd surging about the door. He wore a heavily-furred overcoat, which he did not attempt to remove, though the atmosphere was oppressively close.

46

As he made his way up the room and took his place at the table, a peculiar stillness became apparent. It originated with those in the immediate neighbourhood of the chair, and passed like a magnetic wave over the entire audience. Gradually the indeterminate hum of voices dropped, wavered, and died away. When Curtis Yorke rose to address the meeting, he was received in absolute silence.

The speech which followed was the most remarkable piece of oratory ever delivered at a company's meeting. It comprised the entire history of the San Sacrada Gold Mine, with details and statistics, several of which, unknown at the time even to the directors, were subsequently verified by telegram and proved to be absolutely exact.

Yorke's manner created a profound impression. He spoke for an hour without a single hesitation, and he held his hearers spell-bound. Not an argument was wasted, not a point lost, not a possible objection left unanswered. The man was transfigured by his intense earnestness. His face was inspired, his whole person dilated. He predicted the future success of the company with the authority of one who *knew*. Every word he uttered carried conviction; and when at last a vote of confidence in the Board was put to the meeting, it was carried without a single dissentient. Then an odd thing happened.

Without a word, the chairman rose and left the room. The crowd fell back, making a way for him to the door. His disappearance was succeeded by a second of dead silence. Then Fielden, acting on an impulse, for which he could never afterwards account, sprang up and followed.

He wasn't more than a minute in gaining the stairs; but when he reached the passage Yorke was nowhere to be seen.

He hurried out on to the pavement.

A brougham had just pulled up at the kerb, and someone called him by name.

It was the doctor whom Yorke was in the habit of consulting.

He said something, the drift of which Fielden did not catch, for he was looking up and down the street, and answered by the question uppermost in his mind—

"Have you seen Yorke?"

The reply was startling.

"Yes, poor fellow; but there was nothing to be done. He must have been dead for hours. His servant begged me to come to you. He says there are some important papers which you—"

"What the deuce are you talking about?" Fielden interrupted impatiently. "Yorke's no more dead than I am. He has been at the meeting since three o'clock. He has only just this minute left. I followed him downstairs."

Then, catching the peculiar expression of the medical man's face, he added warmly—

"I'm neither mad nor drunk, Dr. Jones. If you don't believe me, go upstairs. The whole meeting's there, reporters and all. Ask them who took the chair this afternoon. Dead men don't make such speeches as Yorke has just given us."

There was no doubting the sincerity of his tones.

Dr. Jones considered a moment; then he asked a rather singular question—

"Did you," he said, "speak to Mr. Yorke yourself?"

"No; he left the room suddenly, without addressing anyone individually. I thought the strain had been too much for him—he had spoken really magnificently—and I followed, but—"

"Ah!" interjected the other softly; "I think, Mr. Fielden, I must ask you to come back with me. There are papers about of which you, as an intimate personal friend of Yorke's and a representative of the company, had better take charge. Besides, you may be able to elucidate—"

"Do you," said Fielden, "seriously expect me to believe in the death of a man whom I have seen within the last five minutes?"

"I expect nothing. I merely tell you that Mr. Yorke was found dead in his room at half-past two this afternoon. He had given orders overnight that he was not to be disturbed until he rang; but his servant, knowing he was to attend an important meeting at three o'clock, became uneasy, and, after repeated attempts to obtain admission, broke open the door and found his master as I have said. The man at once sent for me, also for Dr. Lewis, of Harley Street; but, of course, there was nothing to be done. Mr. Yorke must have been dead for at least five hours. The body was quite cold. The cause of death was cerebral apoplexy, brought on by nervous pressure and prolonged mental strain. I have known for some days that he was in a serious condition of health."

The brougham rolled noiselessly on its way. Fielden was staggered. His mind refused to take in the full meaning of the doctor's words. Neither man spoke again till the carriage drew up at the chambers which Yorke occupied. His servant was waiting for them in the hall, and led the way upstairs. The bedroom was in disorder; the candles had burned down in their sockets; papers were scattered over the writing-table and floor.

On the bed, which had not been occupied during the night, lay the dead body of Curtis Yorke.

"He was found here," said the doctor, indicating the writing-table. "Evidently he was working up to—the end."

Fielden had been standing by the bed, reverently looking down at the still face on the pillow. The door of a wardrobe opposite had swung back. As he raised his head, his eyes fell upon Yorke's fur-lined overcoat, and the events of the afternoon came back upon him in all their weird improbability. He crossed the room and laid a shaking hand on the doctor's arm.

"What does it mean?" he asked hoarsely. "What does it mean? I saw him, I tell you, not half an hour ago. I heard him speak, and yet—he is dead. For God's sake, what *does* it mean?"

"I don't know," the other answered, simply. "There are some things that won't bear explanation. The affairs of the company were very much on his mind and, turning over the papers lying on the table, he added: "He was preparing his speech when the end came. Look here; is this anything like what you heard?"

Fielden looked, and a smothered exclamation escaped his lips as he glanced down the closely-written pages. He was reading, word for word, the speech to which he had listened barely an hour before.

The eyes of the two men met, and Fielden nodded. There was a pause, broken only by the rattle of a passing cab. A corner of the hearthrug was turned up, and the doctor stooped mechanically to straighten it. Under the fold lay a piece of paper. It had dropped from the dead man's hand and remained there unnoticed since the removal of the body.

Fielden heard his companion draw in his breath with a soft, sibilant sound, and looked up.

"What is it?" he asked.

"Convincing proof, if any were needed, of that poor fellow's mental condition. Good God! what a strain he must have been running under before things got to this pass. Read it for yourself. What do you make of it?"

Fielden read, and there came back to his mind the words Yorke had spoken in the boardroom four days before—

"I am prepared to sell my soul for that end, and I believe the sale will shortly be concluded."

It was the last copy of that extraordinary document by which the unhappy man believed he had saved the San Sacrada Mining Company and lost his own soul.

On the back of the paper Yorke had written:—

My friend Fielden has said that there is no demand for souls nowadays—that they are altogether too cheap—but he is wrong. The devil is never weary of bringing men to destruction, as I am proving, at what cost is known only to myself. Though I am now past hope in this world or the next, I solemnly swear that I did not seriously intend to register this shameful bargain with the powers of darkness.

In a moment of abstraction, hardly knowing what I did, I wrote out the original of this agreement. Three minutes later *it was signed*, and I knew that I was lost.

I saw the vile name come out in letters of fire—the fire of hell, in which my soul, that I have bartered away, must burn hereafter.

Six times I have destroyed the outward evidence of this cursed bone, only to be compelled, by a power stronger than myself, to reproduce it, and watch the awful signature again affixed. *His* share of the compact will soon be completed. My part is yet to come. The surrender of my soul 'at such time and for such purpose.' The purpose I know only too well. The time is yet uncertain, but I feel that it will not be long. I am now tormented by one terrible fear; that the call may come before I have seen the success of the company assured; that after all I may be cheated out of my dearly-bought triumph.

But that I am resolved not to suffer. Surely my body will have strength to resist; my will-power suffice to claim that last privilege. Come what may, I *will not* yield up my immortal self before Friday's meeting. After that I care little how soon the summons comes. This hourly suspense is torture, worse than any actual suffering. My brain is burning already. My mind is already in hell. But—

Here the writing ceased, with a faint downward stroke of the pen, as it had slipped through the nerveless fingers.

It was Curtis Yorke's last word.

The summons had come.

Fielden's eyes were wet as he finished reading.

"Poor fellow," he said under his breath. "Poor Yorke. My God!

What he must have gone through!"

He turned the paper over, and looked at the strangely worded agreement.

The space left for the signature was blank.

This is the truth of a story to which no one will give credence, least of all the hundred and fifty odd men who heard Yorke's speech at the general meeting of the San Sacrada Mining Company. They will prefer to believe that two competent medical authorities made a mistake of five hours in assigning the time of his death. For there is nothing to which human nature objects so strongly as contact with the supernatural, and no credulity equal to the credulity of the incredulous.

In the Séance Room

Dr. Valentine Burke sat alone by the fire. He had finished his rounds, and no patient had disturbed his post-prandial reflections. The house was very quiet, for the servants had gone to bed, and only the occasional rattle of a passing cab and the light patter of the rain on the window-panes broke the silence of the night. The cheerful glow of the fire and the soft light from the yellow-shaded lamp contrasted pleasantly with the dreary fog which filled the street outside. There were spirit-decanters on the table, flanked by a siphon and a box of choice cigars. Valentine Burke liked his creature comforts. The world and the flesh held full measure of attraction for him, but he did not care about working for his *menus plaisirs*.

The ordinary routine of his profession bored him. That he might eventually succeed as a ladies' doctor was tolerably certain. For a young man with little influence and less money, he was doing remarkably well; but Burke was ambitious, and he had a line of his own. He dabbled in psychics, and had written an article on the future of hypnotism, which had attracted considerable attention. He was a strong magnetiser, and offered no objection to semi-private exhibitions of his powers.

In many drawing-rooms he was already regarded as the apostle of the coming revolution which is to substitute disintegration of matter and cerebral precipitation for the present system of the parcels mail and telegraphic communication. In that section of society which interests itself in occultism Burke saw his way to making a big success.

Meanwhile, as man cannot live on adulation alone, the doctor had a living to get, and he had no intention whatever of getting it by the labour of his hands. He was an astute young man, who knew how to invest his capital to the best advantage. His good looks were his capital, and he was about to invest them in a wealthy marriage. The fates had certainly been propitious when they brought Miss Elma Lang into the charmed circle of the Society for the Revival of Eastern Mysticism.

Miss Lang was an orphan. She had full control of her fortune of thirty thousand pounds. She was young, sufficiently pretty, and extremely susceptible. Burke saw his chance, and went for it, to such good purpose that before a month had passed his engagement to the heiress was announced, and the wedding-day within measurable distance.

There were several other candidates for Miss Lang's hand, but it soon became evident that the doctor was first favourite. The gentlemen who devoted themselves to occultism for the most part despised physical attractions; their garments were fearfully and wonderfully made. They were careless as to the arrangement of their hair. Beside them, Valentine Burke, handsome, well set up, and admirably turned out, showed to the very greatest advantage. Elma Lang adored him. She was never tired of admiring him. She was lavish of pretty tokens of her regard. Her photographs, in costly frames, were scattered about his room, and on his hand glittered the single-stone diamond ring which had been her betrothal gift.

He smiled pleasantly as he watched the firelight glinting from the many-coloured facets. "I have been lucky," he said aloud; "I pulled that through very neatly. Just in time, too, for my credit would not stand another year. I ought to be all right now if—." He broke off abruptly', and the smile died away. "If it were not for that other unfortunate affair! What a fool—what a d——d fool I was not to let the girl alone, and what a fool she was to trust me! Why could she not have taken better care of herself? Why could not the old man have looked after her? He made row enough over shutting the stable-door when the horse was gone. It was cleverly' managed though. I think even *ce cher papa* exonerates me from any participation in her disappearance; and fate seems to be playing into my hand too. That body turning up just now is a stroke of luck. I wonder who the poor devil really is?"

He felt for his pocketbook, and took out a newspaper cutting. It was headed in large type, "Mysterious Disappearance of a Young Lady":—

The body found yesterday by the police in Muddlesham Harbour is believed to be that of Miss Katharine Greaves, whose mysterious disappearance in January last created so great a sensation. It will be remembered that Miss Greaves, who was a daughter of a well-known physician at Templeford, Worcestershire, had gone to Muddlesham on a visit to her married sister, from whose house she suddenly disappeared. Despite the most strenuous efforts on the part of her distracted family, backed by the assistance of able detectives, her fate has up to the present remained enshrouded in mystery. On the recovery of the body yesterday the Muddlesham police at once communicated with the relations of Miss Greaves, by whom the clothing was identified. It is now supposed that the unhappy girl threw herself into the harbour during a fit of temporary insanity, resulting, it is believed, from an unfortunate love affair.

Valentine Burke read the paragraph through carefully, and replaced it in the pocketbook with a cynical smile.

"How exquisitely credulous are the police, and the relatives, and the noble British public. Poor Kitty is practically dead—to the world. What a pity—" He hesitated, and stared into the blazing coals. "It would save so much trouble," he went on after a pause, "and I hate trouble."

His fingers were playing absently with a letter from which he had taken the slip of printed paper—an untidy letter, blotted and smeared, and hastily written on poor, thin paper He looked at it once or twice and tossed it into the fire. The note-sheet shrivelled and curled over, dropping on to the hearth, where it lay smouldering. A hot cinder had fallen out of the grate, and the doctor, stretching out his foot, kicked the letter closer to the live coal. Little red sparks crept like glow-worms along the scorched edges flickered and died out. The paper would not ignite; it was damp—damp with a woman's tears.

"I was a fool," he murmured, with conviction. "It was not good enough, and it might have ruined me." He turned to the spirit-stand and replenished his glass, measuring the brandy carefully. "I don't know that I am out of the wood yet," he went on, as he filled up the tumbler with soda-water. "The money is running short, and women are so d——d inconsiderate. If Kitty were to take it into her head to turn up here it would be the—" The sentence remained unfinished, cut short by a sound from below. Someone had rung the night-bell.

Burke set down the glass and bent forward, listening intently. The ring, timid, almost deprecating, was utterly unlike the usual imperative summons for medical aid. Following immediately on his outspoken thoughts, it created an uncomfortable impression of coming danger. He felt certain that it was not a patient; and if it were not a patient, who was it? There was a balcony to the window. He stepped quietly out and leaned over the railing. By the irregular flicker of the street-lamp he could make out the dark figure of a woman on the steps beneath, and through the patter of the falling rain he fancied he caught the sound of a suppressed sob.

With a quick glance, to assure himself that no one was in sight, the doctor ran downstairs and opened the door. A swirl of rain blew into the lighted hall. The woman was leaning against one of the pillars apparently unconscious. Burke touched her shoulder. "What are you doing here?" he asked sharply. At the sound of his voice she uttered a little cry and made a sudden step forward, stumbling over the threshold, and falling heavily against him.

"Val, Val," she cried, despairingly, "I thought I should never find you. Take me home, take me home. I am so tired—and, oh, so frightened!"

The last word died away in a wailing sob, then her hands relaxed their dinging hold and dropped nervelessly at her side.

In an emergency Dr. Burke acted promptly. He shut the outer door, and gathering up the fainting girl in his arms, carried her into the consulting-room, and laid her on the sofa. There was no touch of tenderness in his handling of the unconscious form. He had never cared much about her, when at her best, dainty in figure and fair of face; he had made love to her, *pour passer le temps*, in the dullness of a small country town.

She had met him more than halfway, and almost before his caprice was gratified, he was weary of her. Her very devotion nauseated him. He looked at her now with a shudder of repulsion. The gaslight flared coldly, on the white face, drawn by pain and misery. All its pretty youthfulness had vanished. The short hair, uncurled by the damp night air straggled over the thin forehead. There were lines about the closed eyes and the drooping corners of the mouth. The skin was strained tightly over the cheek-bones and looked yellow, like discoloured wax.

His eyes noted every defect of face and figure, as he stood wondering what he should do with her. He knew, no one better, how quickly the breath of scandal can injure a professional man. Once let the real story of his relations with Katharine Greaves get wind and his career would be practically ruined. He began to realise the gravity of the situation. Two futures lay before him. The one, bright with the sunshine of love and prosperity; the other darkened by poverty and disgrace. He pictured himself the husband of Elma Lang, with all the advantages accruing to the possessor of a charming wife and a large fortune, and he cursed fate which had sent this wreck of womanhood to stand between him and happiness.

By this time, she had partially recovered, and her eyes opened with the painful upward roll common to nervous patients when regaining consciousness. With her dishevelled hair and rain-soaked garments, she had all the appearance of a dead body. The sight, horrible as it was, fascinated Burke. He turned up the gas, twisting the chandelier so as to throw a full light on the girl's face.

"She looks as though she were drowned," he thought. "When she is really dead, she will look like that" The idea took possession of his mind. "If she were dead, if only she were really dead!"

Who can trust the discretion of a wronged and forsaken woman, but—the dead tell no tales. If only she were dead! The words repeated themselves again and again, beating into his brain like the heavy strokes of a hammer. Why should she not die? Her life was over, a spoiled, ruined thing.

There was nothing before her but shame and misery. She would be better dead. Why (he laughed suddenly a hard, mirthless laugh), she was dead already. Her body had been found by the police, identified by her own relations. She was supposed to be drowned, why not make the supposition a reality? A curious light flashed into the doctor's handsome face. A woman seeing him at that moment would have hesitated before trusting her life in his hands. He looked at his unwelcome visitor with an evil smile.

She had come round now and was crouched in the corner of the sofa sobbing and shivering.

"Don't be angry with me, Val, please don't be angry. I waited till I had only just enough money for my ticket, and I dare not stay there any longer. It is so lonely, and you never come to see me now. It is ten weeks since you were down, and you won't answer my letters. I was so frightened all alone. I began to think you were getting tired of me. Of course, I know it is all nonsense. You love me as much as you ever did. It is only that you are so busy and hate writing letters." She paused, waiting for some reassuring words, but he did not answer, only watched her with cold, steady eyes.

"Did you see the papers," she went on, with chattering teeth. "They think I am dead. Ever since I read it, I have had such dreadful thoughts. I keep seeing myself drowned; I believe I am going to die, Val—and I don't want to die. I am so—so frightened. I thought you would take me in your arms and comfort me like you used to do, and I should feel safe. Oh, why don't you speak to me? Why do you look at me like that? Val, dear, don't do it, *don't* do it, I cannot bear it."

Her great terrified eyes were fixed on his, fascinated by his steady, unflinching gaze. She was trembling violently. Her words came with difficulty, in short gasps.

"You have never said you were glad to see me. It is true, then, that you don't love me anymore. You are tired of me, and you will not marry me now. What shall I do? what shall I do? No one cares for me, no one wants me, and there is nothing left for me but to die."

Still no answer. There was a long silence while their eyes met in that fixed stare—his cold, steady, dominating, hers flinching and striving vainly to withstand the power of the stronger will. In a few moments the unequal struggle had ended. The girl sat stiff and erect, her hand grasping the arm of the sofa. The light of consciousness had died out of the blue eyes, leaving them fixed and glassy. Burke crossed the floor and stood in front of her.

"Where is your luggage?" he asked, authoritatively."

She answered in a dull, mechanical way, "At the station."

"Have you kept anything marked with your own name—any of my letters?"

"No, nothing—there."

"You *have* kept some of my letters. Where are they?"

"Here." Her hand sought vaguely for her pocket.

"Give them to me—all of them."

Mechanically she obeyed him, holding out three envelopes, after separating them carefully from her purse and handkerchief.

"Give me the other things." He opened the purse. Besides a few shillings, it contained only a visiting-card, on which an address had been written in pencil. The doctor tore the card across and tossed it into the fireplace. Then his eyes fastened on those of the girl before him. Very slowly he bent forward and whispered a few words in her ear, repeating them again and again. The abject terror visible in her face would have touched any heart but that of the man in whose path she stood. No living soul, save the "sensitive" on whom he was experimenting, heard those words, but they were registered by a higher power than that of the criminal court, damning evidence to be produced one day against the man who had prostituted his spiritual gift to mean and selfish ends.

In the grey light of the chilly November morning a park-keeper, near the Regent's Canal, was startled by a sudden, piercing shriek. Hurrying in the direction of the sound, he saw, through the leafless branches, a figure struggling in the black water. The park-keeper was a plucky fellow, whose courage had gained more than one recognition from the Humane Society, and he began to run towards the spot where that dark form had been, but before he had covered ten yards of ground rapid footsteps gained on his and a man shot past him. "Someone in the canal," he shouted as he ran. "I think it is a woman. You had better get help."

"He was a good plucked one," the park-keeper averred, when a few days later he retailed the story to a select circle of friends at the bar of the "Regent's Arms," where the inquest had been held. "Not that I'd have been behindhand, but my wind ain't what it was, and he might have been shot out of a catapult He was off with his coat and into the water before you could say Jack Robinson. Twice I thought he had her safe enough, and twice she pulled him under; the third time, blest if I thought they were coming up any more at all. Then the doctor chap, he comes to the surface dead-beat, but the girl in his arms.

"'I'm afraid she's gone,' he says, when I took her from him, 'but we won't lose time,' and he set to and carried out all the instructions for recovering the apparently drowned while I went for some brandy. It wasn't a bit of use. The young woman were as dead as a doornail. 'If she'd only have kept quiet, I might have saved her,' he says, quite sorrowful like, 'but she struggled so,' and sure enough his hands were regularly torn and bruised where she'd gripped him."

Dr. Burke and the park-keeper were the chief witnesses at the inquest. There were no means of identifying the dead woman. The jury returned a verdict of *felo de se,* and the coroner complimented the doctor on his courageous attempt to rescue the poor outcast.

The newspapers, too, gave him a nice little paragraph, headed, "Determined Suicide in Regent's Park. Gallant conduct of a well-known physician;" and Elma Lang's dark eyes filled with fond and happy tears as she read her lover's praises.

"You are so brave, Val, so good," she cried, "and I am so proud of you; but you ran a horrible risk."

"Yes," he answered, gravely, "I thought once it was all up with me. That poor girl nearly succeeded in drowning the pair of us. Still, there wasn't much in it, you know; any other fellow would have done the same."

"No, they would not. It is no use trying to pretend you are not a hero, Val, because you are. How awful it must have been when she clung to you so desperately. It might have cost you your life."

"It cost me my ring," he replied, ruefully. "It is lying at the bottom of the canal at this moment, unless some adventurous fish has swallowed it—your first gift."

"What does it matter," she answered, impulsively, "I can give you another tomorrow. What does anything matter since you are safe?"

Burke took her in his arms, and kissed the pretty upturned face. She was his now, bought with the price of another woman's life. Bah! he wanted to forget the clutch of those stiffening fingers and the glazed awful stare of the dead eyes through the water.

"Let us drop the subject," he said, gently. "It is not a pleasant one, and, as you say, nothing matters since I am safe"—he added under his breath, "quite safe *now*."

****

The carriage stood at the door. In the drawing-room Mrs. Burke was waiting for her husband. She had often waited for the doctor during the four years which had elapsed since their marriage. Those four years had seen to a great extent the fulfilment of Burke's ambition. He had money. He was popular, sought after, an acknowledged leader of the new school of Philosophy, an authority on psychic phenomena, and the idol of the "smart" women who played with the fashionable theories and talked glibly on subjects the very ABC of which was far beyond their feeble comprehension.

Socially, Dr. Burke was an immense success. If, as a husband, he fell short of Elma's expectations, she never admitted the fact. She made an admirable wife, interesting herself in his studies, and assisting him materially in his literary work. Outwardly, they were a devoted couple. The world knew nothing of the indefinable barrier which held husband and wife apart; of a certain vague distrust which had crept into the woman's heart, bred of an instinctive feeling that her husband was not what he seemed to be. Something, she knew not what, lay between them. Her quick perceptions told her that he was always acting a part.

She held in her hand a little sheaf of papers, notes that she had prepared for him on the series of *séances*, which for a month past had been the talk of the town. A medium of extraordinary power had flashed like a meteor into the firmament of London society. Phenomena of the most startling kind had baffled alike the explanations of both scientist and occultist. Spiritualism was triumphant. A test committee had been formed, of which Dr. Burke was unanimously elected president, but so far, the attempts to expose the alleged frauds had not been attended with any success.

It was to Mdme. Delphine's house that the Burkes were going tonight. The *séance* commenced at ten, and the hands of the clock already pointed to a quarter to that hour, when the doctor hurried into the room.

"Ready?" he said. "Come along then. Where are the notes?"

He glanced hastily through them as he went downstairs.

"Falconer and I have been there all the afternoon," he explained as they drove off. "I had only just time to get something to eat at the club before I dressed. We have taken the most elaborate precautions. If something cannot be proved tonight—" He paused.

"Well?" she said, anxiously.

"We shall be the laughing-stock of London," he concluded, emphatically.

"What do you really think of it?"

"Humbug, of course; but the difficulty is to prove it."

"Mrs. Thirlwall declares that the fifth appearance last night was undoubtedly her husband. I saw her today; she was quite overcome."

"Mrs. Thirlwall is an hysterical fool."

"But your theory admitted the possibility of materialising the intense mental—"

Burke leaned back in the carriage, laughing softly.

"My dear child, I had to say something."

"Valentine," she cried, sorrowfully, "is there no truth in anything you say or write? Do you believe in nothing?"

"Certainly. I believe in matter and myself; also, that the many fools exist for the benefit of a minority with brains. When I see any reason to alter my belief, I shall not hesitate to do so. If, for instance, I am convinced that I see with my material eyes a person whom I know to be dead, I will become a convert to spiritualism. But I shall never see it."

The drawing-room was filled when they arrived at Mdme. Delphine's. Seats had been kept for the doctor and his wife. There was a short whispered consultation between Burke and his colleagues, the usual warning from the medium that the audience must conform to the rules of the *séance*, and the business of the evening began in the customary style.

Musical instruments sounded in different parts of the room, light fingers touched the faces of the sitters. Questions written on slips of paper and placed in a sealed cabinet received answers from the spirit world, which the inquirers admitted to be correct. The medium's assistant handed one of these blank slips to Burke, requesting him to fill it up.

It struck the doctor that if he were to ask some question the answer to which he did not himself know, but could afterwards verify, he would guard against the possibility of playing into the hands of an adroit thought-reader. He accordingly wrote on the paper,:

What was I doing this time four years ago? Give the initials of my companions, if any.

He had not the vaguest idea as to where exactly he had been on the date in question, but a reference to the rough diary he always kept would verify or disprove the answer.

The folded slip was sealed and placed in the cabinet.

In due time the medium declared the replies were ready. The cabinet was opened, and the slips, numbered in the order in which they had been given in, were returned to their owners. Burke noticed that there were no fresh folds in his paper, and the seal was of course unbroken. He opened it, and as his eye fell on the writing, he gave a slight start, and glanced sharply at the medium. Beneath his query was written in ink that was scarcely yet dry:

On Wednesday, November, 17, 1885, you were at No. 63, Abbey Road. I only was with you. You hypnotised me.—K. G.

The handwriting was that of Katharine Greaves.

The doctor was staggered. In the multiplied interests and distractions of his daily life he had completely forgotten the date of that tragic visit. He tried to recall the exact day of the month and week. He remembered now that it was on a Wednesday, and this was Monday. Calculating the odd days for the leap year, 1888, that would bring it to Monday—Monday, the 17th. Four years ago tonight Kitty had been alive. She was dead now, and yet here before him was a paper written in her hand. He sat staring at the characters, lost in thought. The familiar writing brought back with irresistible force the memory of that painful interview. It suggested another and very serious danger.

Burke did not believe for a moment that the answer to his question had been dictated by the disembodied spirit of his victim. He was racking his brains to discover how his secret might possibly have leaked out, who this woman could be who knew, and traded on her knowledge, of that dark passage in his life which he had believed to be hidden from all the world. Was it merely a bow drawn at a venture, which had chanced to strike the one weak place in his armour, or was it deliberately planned with a view to extorting money?

So deeply was he wrapped in his reflections, that the manifestations went on around him unheeded. The dark curtain which screened off a portion of the room divided, and a white-robed child stepped out. It was instantly recognised by one of the sitters—a nervous, highly-strung woman, whose passionate entreaties that her dead darling would return to earth fairly harrowed the feelings of the listeners. Other manifestations followed. The audience were becoming greatly excited. Burke sat indifferent to it all, his eyes fixed on the writing before him, till his wife touched him gently.

"What is the matter, Val?" she whispered, trying to read the paper over his shoulder. "Is your answer correct?"

He turned on her sharply, crushing the message in his hand. "No," he said audibly. "It is a gross imposture. There was no such person."

"Hush." She laid a restraining hand on his arm. "Do not speak so loudly. That is a point in our favour, anyway. Mr. Falconer has proposed a fresh test. He has asked if a material object, something that had been lost at any time, you know, can be restored by the spirits. *Madame* returned a favourable answer. Mr. Falconer could not think of anything at the moment, but I had a brilliant inspiration. I told him to ask for your diamond ring—the ring you lost when you tried to save that poor girl's life."

Burke rose to his feet, then recollecting himself, sat down again and tried to pull himself together. There was nothing in it. If this Madame Delphine was really acquainted with the facts of his relations with Katharine Greaves, she could not know its ghastly termination. He tried to reassure himself, but vainly. His nerve was deserting him, and his eyes roved vacantly round the semi-darkened room, as if in search of something. A sudden silence had fallen on the audience. A cold chill, like a draft of icy air, swept through the *séances* chamber. Mrs. Burke shivered from head to foot, and drew closer to her husband. Suddenly the stillness was broken by a shriek of horror.

It issued from the lips of the medium, who, like a second Witch of Endor, saw more than she expected, and crouched terror-stricken in the chair to which she was secured by cords adjusted by the test committee. The presence which had appeared before the black curtain was no white-clad denizen of "summerland," but a woman in dark, clinging garments—garments, to all appearance, dripping with water—a woman with wide-opened, glassy eyes, fixed in an unalterable stony stare. It was a ghastly sight. All the concentrated agony of a violent death was stamped on that awful face.

Of the twenty people who looked upon it, not one had power to move or speak.

Slowly the terrible thing glided forward, hardly touching the ground, one hand outstretched, and on the open palm a small, glittering object—a diamond ring!

It moved very slowly, and the second or so during which it traversed the space between the curtain and the seats of the audience seemed hours to the man who knew for whom it came.

Valentine Burke sat rigid. He was oblivious of the presence of spectators, hardly conscious of his own existence. Everything was swallowed up in a suspense too agonising for words, the fearful expectancy of what was about to happen. Nearer and nearer "it" came. Now it was close to him. He could feel the deathly dampness of its breath; those awful eyes were looking into his. The distorted lips parted—formed a single word. Was it the voice of a guilty conscience, or did that word really ring through and through the room—"Murderer!"

For a full minute the agony lasted, then something fell with a sharp click on the carpetless floor. The sound recalled the petrified audience to a consciousness of mundane things. They became aware that "it" was gone.

They moved furtively, glanced at each other—at last someone spoke. It was Mrs. Burke. She had vainly tried to attract her husband's attention, and now turned to Falconer, who sat next to her.

"Help me to get him away," she said.

The doctor alone had not stirred; his eyes were fixed as though he were still confronted by that unearthly presence.

Someone had turned up the gas. Two of the committee were releasing the medium, who was half dead with fright. Falconer unfastened the door, and seat a servant whom he met in the hall for a hansom.

When he returned to the *séance* room the doctor was still in the same position. It was some moments before he could be roused, but when once they succeeded in their efforts Burke's senses seemed to return. He rose directly, and prepared to accompany his wife. As they quitted their seats, Falconer's eyes fell on the diamond ring which lay unnoticed on the ground. He was going to pick it up, but someone caught his hand and stopped him.

"Leave it alone," said Mrs. Burke, in a horrified whisper. "For God's sake, don't touch it!"

Husband and wife drove home in silence. Silently the doctor dismissed the cab and opened the hall-door. The gas was burning brightly in the study. The servant had left on the side-table a tray with sandwiches, wine, and spirits. Burke poured out some brandy and tossed it off neat. His face was still rather white, otherwise he had quite recovered his usual composure.

Mrs. Burke loosened her cloak and dropped wearily into a chair by the fire. A hopeless despondency was visible in every line of her attitude. Once or twice the doctor looked at her, and opened his lips to speak. Then he thought better of it, and kept silence. Half an hour passed in this way. At last Burke lighted a candle and left the room. When he returned, he carried in his hand a small bottle. He had completely regained his self-possession as he came over to his wife and scrutinised her troubled face.

"Have some wine," he said, "and then you had better go to bed. You look thoroughly done up."

"What is that?" She pointed to the bottle in his hand.

"A sleeping-draught. Merely a little morphia and bromide. I should advise you to take one, too. Frankly, tonight's performance was enough to try the strongest nerves. Mine require steadying by a good night's rest, and I do not intend risking an attack of insomnia."

She rose suddenly from her chair and clasped her hands on his arm.

"Val," she cried, piteously, "don't try to deceive me. Dear, I can bear anything if you will only trust me and tell me the truth. What is this thing which stands between us? What was the meaning of that awful sight?"

For a moment he hesitated; then he pulled himself together and answered lightly—

"My dear girl, you are unnerved, and I do not wonder at it. Let us forget it."

"I cannot, I cannot," she interrupted wildly. "I must know what it meant. I have always felt there was something. Valentine, I beseech you, by everything you hold sacred, tell me the truth now before it is too late. I could forgive you almost—almost anything, if you will tell me bravely; but do not leave me to find it out for myself."

"There is nothing to tell."

"You will not trust me?"

"I tell you there is nothing."

"That is your final answer?"

"Yes."

Without a word she left the room and went upstairs. Burke soon followed her. His nerves had been sufficiently shaken to make solitude undesirable. He smoked a cigar in his dressing-room, and took the sleeping-draught before going to bed. The effects of the opiate lasted for several hours. It was broad daylight when the doctor awoke. He felt weak and used up, and his head was splitting. He lay for a short time in that drowsy condition which is the border-land between sleeping and waking. Then he became conscious that his wife was not in the room. He looked at his watch, and saw that it was half-past nine. He waited a few minutes, expecting her to return, but she did not come. Presently he got up and drew back the window-curtains.

As the full light streamed in, he was struck by a certain change in the appearance of the room. At first, he was uncertain in what the change consisted, but gradually he realised that it lay in the absence of the usual feminine impedimenta. The dressing-table was shorn of its silver toilet accessories. One or two drawers were open and emptied of their contents.

The writing-table was cleared, and his wife's dressing-case had disappeared from its usual place. Burke's first impulse was to ring for a servant and make inquiries, but as he stretched out his hand to the bell his eyes fell on a letter, conspicuously placed on the centre of a small table. It was addressed in Elma's handwriting. From that moment Burke knew that something had happened, and he was prepared for the worst. The letter was not long. It was written firmly, though pale-blue stains here and there indicated where the wet ink had been splashed by failing tears. She wrote:

When you read this, I shall have left you forever. The only reparation in your power is to refrain from any attempt to follow me; indeed, you will hardly desire to do so, when I tell you that I know all. I said last night I could not endure the torture of uncertainty. My fears were so terrible that I felt I must know the truth or die. I implored you to trust me. You put me off with a lie. Was I to blame if I used against you a power which you yourself had taught me? In the last four hours I have heard from your own lips the whole story of Katharine Greaves.

Every detail of that horrible tragedy you confessed unconsciously in your sleep, and I who loved you—Heaven knows how dearly!—have to endure the agony of knowing my husband to be a murderer, and that my wretched fortune supplied the motive for the crime. Thank God that I have no child to bear the curse of your sin, to inherit its father's nature! I hardly know what I am writing. The very ground seems to be cut away from under my feet. On every side I can see nothing but densest darkness, and the only thing that is left to us is death.—
Your wretched wife, Elma.

From the moment he opened the letter, Burke's decision was made. He possessed the exact admixture of physical courage and moral cowardice which induces a man worsted in the battle of life to end the conflict by removing himself from the arena. He had taken the best of the world's gifts, and there was nothing left worth having. His belief in a future life was too vague to cause him any uneasiness, and physically, fear was a word he did not understand. He quietly lighted his wife's letter with a match, and threw it into the fireless grate. He smoked a cigarette while he watched it burn, and carefully hid the charred ashes among the cinders. Then he fetched from his dressing-room a small polished box, unlocked it, and took out the revolver. It was loaded in all six chambers.

Burke leisurely finished his cigarette, and tossed the end away. He never hesitated a moment. He had no regret for the life he was leaving. As Elma had said, there was only one thing left for him to do, and—he did it

The Missing Model

"A plague on all marrying and giving in marriage, say I."

Gordon Mayne flung aside the sheaf of brushes he had been washing and began to stride impatiently up and down the studio.

"Why the deuce does the woman want to get married?" he demanded. "What business has a model to marry at all? She is the property of the artistic public, and no single man should be permitted to monopolise her—least of all a Philistine of a shop-walker who refuses to allow his wife to sit, even to her oldest friend. It is all very well for you to lie grinning there, Faucit; but let me tell you it is no laughing matter. Here am I with an idea, a masterpiece evolving itself in my mind—a picture that should make my name and lift me among the gods on high Olympus; a sublime conception, which I should, of course, have treated sublimely.

"And now, at the eleventh hour, my only model, the one woman who is the living embodiment of my dream, coolly sends me word that she has married a shop-walker—a *shop-walker*, if you please— and can undertake no more engagements. It is absurd! It is brutal! To what end has Nature endowed her with that faultless form and divine length of limb, with that superb carriage, if the one is to be hidden by the stylish abominations of Westbourne Grove clothiers, and the other ruined by wheeling the eternal perambulator down Bayswater slums? Any healthy female of four foot nothing would have answered the purpose equally well. It is sacrilege that—"

"That divine form should be clasped in the arms of a low-born peasant," quoted Faucit from the divan, where he lay luxuriously among the cushions, puffing little clouds of smoke rings into the warm air, and laughing softly at his friend's vehemence. "So it is, old chap. I sympathise. Have a cigarette?"

"I don't care a blue cent who clasps the divine form, so long as I can paint it," retorted the other crossly, ignoring the proffered case;

"but it *is* sacrilege that such a model should be wasted on mere matrimony. I shall never meet her equal! My picture is lost."

"Rot!" responded Faucit, with conviction. "London is stiff with models. There is always as good fish in the sea as ever came out. See here, De Croissac is off to Rome next week. He has a capital girl, 'brunette, statuesque—the reverse of grotesque.' I'll ask him to send her address. You might arrange with her while he is away. He won't be back till October."

The studio was full of the soft gloom of a late afternoon in January. Outside the dying sunset threw a crimson glow on the gathering mists which were turning the prosaic villas of the St. John's Wood Road into enchanted palaces of mystery. Within a wood fire burned between the dogs on the great open hearth and flickered over the unfinished sketches alternating with plaster casts on the walls, over the two or three big easels, and the odds and ends of draperies and Eastern embroideries scattered about. Gordon Mayne had but recently taken possession of the studio. It had been standing empty for some time, and he had secured it at a comparatively low rental.

"It is an odd thing," remarked Faucit, meditatively, "that the very last time I was here Deverill was tearing his hair over the disappearance of a model. You remember his 'Vanity,' don't you? No? Ah, then it was exhibited in '87, when you were in Paris. Well, it was one of the pictures of the year, and the girl who sat for it was lovely, perfectly exquisite. Deverill found her, and she sat to no one but to him and Flint, who is his great chum, you know. One day she did not turn up as usual. It was the first time she had ever failed him, and Deverill fancied something unforeseen had kept her at home, swore a little, and thought no more about it, till late in the evening the girl's father came to inquire at what time his daughter had left the studio. Then it turned out that she had not gone home the previous night, and she never did go home. They searched for her high and low, had the canal dragged, put on detectives, and advertised for weeks, but it wasn't the least use. She had vanished off the face of the earth, and not a word has been heard of her from that day to this."

"Bolted with someone, I suppose," said Mayne, conclusively.

"No, that was the odd part of it. Her name had never been mixed up with a man's. She wasn't that sort of young woman at all. When they searched her room, they found no letters, nothing that gave the smallest clue to any affair of the kind. Besides, she took no clothes with her; absolutely nothing. Deverill was in despair. She was sitting for 'Œnone Forsaken,' the picture he painted for McCandlish, the colonial millionaire, and he had not quite finished it. I can't tell you how much he spent over trying to find her. After that, he threw up the classic, and went in for Scriptural subjects. Queer fellow, Deverill," concluded Faucit, lighting a fresh cigarette. "Would any other man exile himself for three years in some stinking Arab village, for the sake of painting his virgins and disciples on the spot?"

"Lucky for me he went," said Mayne, "or I should have lost the chance of a rattling good studio. Well, if we really mean to dine with Mrs. Lockhart at seven, I must dress. There is some sherry and a bottle of Angostura bitters in that cupboard, and here is a glass. Help yourself while you are waiting. I shall not be long."

Mrs. Lockhart was noted for her little dinners. Covers were invariably laid for eight, and both guests and menu were selected with infinite care. Under the congenial influences of good wine and good company, Mayne forgot his grievances, and it was not till the two men were parting for the night, that he again recurred to the subject of the model. Faucit was going to the club, the artist to St. John's Wood.

"Don't forget to ask for that girl's address," he said, as he stepped into his hansom, and the other nodded assent. In the artistic world Gordon Mayne was generally spoken of as a rising man. He had been rising for several years, without having attained to any considerable height. Not that his work wasn't good, for it was, and the dealers seldom left anything on his hands, but since his first exhibit on the walls of Burlington House he had produced nothing very striking, and the critics, who had prophesied great things of the creator of "Pelagia," felt they had been taken in and let him know it.

By portraits and potboilers a man may gain *lucre*, but not fame; and Gordon had begun to realise that it was high time he should be represented in the summer exhibitions by something more important than young ladies in evening gowns and the pretty green and grey landscapes, with which city gentlemen of artistic predilections like to adorn their suburban dining-rooms. He had waited a long time for an inspiration, and at last the inspiration had come. On the afternoon following Mrs. Lockhart's dinner, Mayne was busily engaged in roughing out his idea with a bit of charcoal, a single female figure—three-quarter-length and life-size—against a curtained doorway. The left hand drew aside the heavy draperies. The right raised the veil from the face.

The picture was to be called "Avenged," and the expression of the woman was to convey its own story to the spectator. If only he could find an adequate model Mayne felt the composition must prove a success. He was sensible of an enthusiasm for the subject which had latterly been wanting in his work, and he was deeply engrossed in the sketch when someone knocked at the outer door—it was a low, almost timid knock, which had to be twice repeated before the artist's attention was fairly arrested. Rather reluctantly he rose to answer the summons. It was almost dark outside, and his eyes, dazzled by the bright light of the studio, took in with difficulty the lineaments of the woman standing on the threshold. She did not speak, only stood looking wistfully into the lighted room.

"You want to see me?" Mayne inquired courteously. "Will you come in?"

He threw back the door. As she stepped forward, he saw that his visitor was a young woman, considerably above the average height, and that she moved superbly, with the natural grace of a perfectly-formed and healthy girl.

A second glance assured him that she was undeniably pretty. She was well, but not fashionably, dressed in some black clinging material which hung in straight, almost classical folds. As she reached the centre of the room she turned and threw back the veil she wore with a gesture that brought an involuntary exclamation to the painter's lips. It was the precise action he had attributed to the figure in his sketch. His eyes devoured the faultless features, the exquisite colouring of the face before him, the rich tint of the chestnut hair visible beneath her hat, the expression of the wonderful eyes. For a few moments he stood silently gazing, lost in admiration of her singular beauty. Then, finding she made no effort to explain her errand, he became conscious of the absurdity of the situation.

"You wish to see me?" he said. "What can I do for you?"

Her eyes rested on the unfinished sketch, as she answered in a low voice—

"You require a model?"

It flashed across Mayne that this must be the girl Faucit had mentioned, and he inwardly endorsed his friend's encomiums on De Croissac's *protégée*. He began at once to explain his requirements, hours, &c. She listened quietly, answering his direct questions, but never volunteering a remark. When the arrangements were completed, she declined his offer of refreshment and went to the door. As he showed her out, the young man reminded her that he knew neither her name nor address. The girl raised her beautiful eyes slowly to his face.

72

"I shall be here at ten," she answered, and slipped past him into the darkness.

Later in the evening a telegram was delivered at the studio. It was from Faucit, stating that he was on the point of starting for Athens, in consequence of a despatch apprising him of the sudden death at the British Embassy of his eldest brother.

Mayne threw himself heart and soul into his new work. The model proved an admirable sitter. She caught the spirit not only of the pose, but of the facial expression, and her powers of endurance were remarkable. She could stand for almost any length of time without evincing the slightest fatigue. As the work grew under his hand, Mayne became more and more fascinated. His artistic sensibilities were roused to a species of exaltation. The picture was never absent from his thoughts by day, and all night long he dreamed of it. The singular beauty of his model exercised over him an almost magnetic influence.

The hours he spent with her in the studio were like an introduction into a new and unknown world. Without analysing the cause, he was conscious in her presence of a keen delight to which he had hitherto been a stranger. He was jealous of any eye but his resting on that exquisite face, and denied himself to all visitors during the sittings. He worked for the most part in silence. The girl never spoke unless directly addressed. She was surrounded by an atmosphere of mystery. She showed the strongest aversion to meeting with strangers, and on two occasions on which in the early days of her engagement Mayne had received friends, she disappeared and did not return until he was again alone.

It was not until after she had been sitting to him for several weeks that the artist learned her name and address, and then only on condition that he should make no use of his knowledge except under urgent necessity. He gave the promise readily, as he would have agreed to anything she required, for she had obtained a remarkable influence over the young man. Without a word having passed between them, he was deeply in love with his model, and he believed that she understood his unexpressed sentiment towards her.

At the end of April Faucit returned to town. Family affairs had detained him abroad far into February, after which he had accompanied a relative on a protracted yachting trip. One of his first visits was paid to the studio in St. John's Wood. He found Mayne at home, and disengaged. The two men had not corresponded, and Faucit inquired with interest after the progress of his friend's work.

"How did you manage about your model?" he asked, when he had settled himself on the divan and lighted the usual cigarette. "I thought once of writing to De Croissac about that girl, but I didn't know his address in Rome, and the news of poor Bob's death drove everything else out of my head before I left England."

Mayne stared at him blankly.

"But you did send her," he said. "She came the very next day."

"She—who?"

"The model, of course; and I can never thank you sufficiently for what you did for me. She is an inspiration. I can honestly say that picture is the best thing I have ever done. It is splendidly hung, on line at the end of the second room. See here," he pointed to the black-and-white study which hung on the opposite wall; "that gives you a faint idea of it."

Faucit pulled himself up, and went over to the sketch. As his eyes rested on it his face changed.

"Good God!" he exclaimed, "who sat for that?"

"De Croissac's model, the girl you sent, and the most perfect woman in the whole world."

"Are you off your head?" cried Faucit; "that is no more De Croissac's model than I am, and I never sent anyone. That is—Great Heavens! Mayne, don't play the fool. Where did you find her? How did she get here? Answer me," as the artist stood in silent amazement at this unprecedented outburst of excitement on the part of his impassive friend, "where in the name of all that is wonderful did you come across Violet Lucas?"

"You know her name?"

"Know her name," repeated the other impatiently. "Wasn't her name advertised in every paper, at every police station in London. I tell you the original of that picture is none other than Deverill's lost model, the girl who disappeared three years ago."

★★★★★★★★

The private view of the Royal Academy was, if anything, more largely attended than usual. All sorts and conditions of notabilities thronged the principal rooms. Lady journalists taking hasty notes of the costume worn by a charming young duchess who was making a tour of inspection under the President's guidance. A leading scientist was arm in arm with a well-known writer of burlesque; R.A.'s and A.R.A.'s by the dozen, stars of the artistic and dramatic firmament, authors, critics, a mammoth picture-dealer, a host of people merely smart, and a smaller sprinkling of those who could not boast even that most modern of all claims to notoriety.

"Very fine picture. Long way the strongest thing we have seen of yours since 'Pelagia.'" The great dealer nodded approvingly at Mayne, who stood chatting with Faucit at a short distance from his work. "I said just now to McCandlish (he's the man for you), 'if you want to see the picture of the year,' I said, 'there it is. Mayne is a coming man. If you don't take it I shall.' Don't you let him have it a penny under six hundred. I'll give five hundred myself for it any day; it's a very fine work."

"Yes," put in the critic of a leading journal, who was also an old friend of the artist, "it takes a lot of punishment to make you try, old man, but when you are screwed up to the point, you are capable of cutting down your field. I've had my knife into you consistently for about four years now, and at last I have succeeded in driving you to produce a picture worth criticising."

"Here is McCandlish," said Bignold, "You don't know him, I think?"

He turned to the newcomer with a few words of explanation, and presented Mayne. The millionaire was a big man, verging on fifty, with immense shoulders and a fresh-coloured, rather sensual face.

He acknowledged the introduction in a somewhat offhand manner, and glanced at the picture. The eyes of three of the little group turned in the same direction; but Faucit, who happened to be looking at the Australian, saw him give an irrepressible start.

"When was this picture painted, Mr. Mayne?" he asked, in a tone that was a trifle too casual.

"I finished it three weeks ago."

"Did you work from a—a model?"

"Certainly, and it is a very faithful portrait."

McCandlish could not take his eyes off the canvas. It had evidently made a great impression on him. With an attempt at carelessness which was not lost on one at least of his auditors, he continued—

"The picture bears a striking resemblance to one already in my possession, but the lady who sat for that is dead, I am told."

"Perhaps"—to his dying day Faucit will never know what prompted the remark—"Miss Lucas is not dead. Perhaps before long she may be—"

"Avenged," said a clear voice at his elbow, "No. 112."

The lady who had spoken passed on, but Faucit, turning, saw that every vestige of colour had died out of the Australian's face. His jaw dropped, his eyes were staring straight before him, where, close by the barrier, stood a tall, graceful woman, dressed in black. With her right hand she raised the veil she wore, and disclosed the exquisite features of Mayne's mysterious model— the original of the picture behind her—the missing Violet Lucas!

For a brace of seconds Faucit held his breath. Then he caught sight of Mayne's face, beaming with delight, and knew that he was not dreaming. With a stifled cry of "My God!" McCandlish staggered back and clung to Bignold's arm for support.

The exclamation distracted Faucit's attention; when he looked again for the girl she was gone. Mayne had also vanished among the crowd, and Bignold, with consternation written on his broad, red face, was inquiring of the colonial what the deuce was the matter with him? McCandlish looked ghastly.

"It is nothing," he stammered; "sort of attack I have sometimes— over directly. Help me to get out of this. The heat is stifling."

The good-natured dealer shouldered a passage through the crowd.

Faucit turned to the critic.

"Did you see that girl?" he asked.

"The one in green? Hardly a girl—forty if she is a day, but a handsome woman still."

"No, no," impatiently; "the girl in black who was standing in front of Mayne's picture."

The other stared.

"Is it a riddle?" he inquired. "I'm not good at riddles. Ask me another."

"You must have seen her," Faucit urged. "It was Mayne's model. What is the joke?" he added, shortly, as his companion broke into a broad smile.

"My dear chap, if it were anyone but you, I should ask where you had been lunching."

"I don't know what the devil you mean," was the retort. "The girl *was* there. McCandlish saw her, so did Mayne, so must you unless you are blind. She was standing *there*," indicating the spot.

The other man instantly became grave.

"You have been overdoing it a little," he said. "I know the sort of thing I get it myself sometimes. Go and see your doctor and take it easy for a bit."

"Do you think I am mad or drunk?" said Faucit, indignantly.

"Neither; but a little overworked. On my honour, old man, there was no one there."

Without another word Faucit left him. Elbowing his way to the door, he met Bignold.

"Where is McCandlish?" he asked.

"I've put him into a cab and sent him home. He seemed all right when I got him outside. Queer sort of attack, wasn't it?"

"Very," Faucit assented, dryly. "The sight of that girl startled him, I suppose."

"What girl?"

The situation was becoming critical. The young man pulled himself together.

"Did you not see," he inquired, trying hard to keep his temper, "a woman in black, standing before Mayne's picture?"

"What the deuce are you driving at? I was straight opposite the picture, and there wasn't any woman that I saw."

There was no mistaking the sincerity of his tone. Faucit muttered something about a mistake, and went in search of Mayne. He found the artist returning breathless from the hall.

"I cannot find her anywhere," he began. "I have been through all the rooms and out into the street. I asked the constable downstairs, but no one seems to have seen her. It is very odd."

"Very odd, indeed," was Faucit's answer. "Come outside, where we can talk quietly. There is more in this than meets the eye."

"Look here," was his next remark, when he had related what had passed during Mayne's absence. "There is a screw loose somewhere. I do not believe in spiritualism and that sort of thing, but I mean to get to the bottom of this business. You say Miss Lucas gave you her address; you must communicate with her."

"But," objected Mayne, "she said I could not see her for three weeks, and I promised not to use the address except under urgent necessity."

"The necessity is urgent. I met Flint last night, and he told me (I was making inquiries about her) that Miss Lucas's people know nothing of her whereabouts. They believe her to be dead. Now she was a good girl, and devoted to her father and sister; if she were living in town, a free agent, would she keep them in ignorance of her fate?"

"Then you think—?"

"Never mind what I think. What is her address?"

"Alma Cottage, St. Cyr Road, Hampstead. Shall I write?"

"No," said Faucit, "we will go. You shall see her while I wait in the cab. If she is not at home you can write tonight."

They hailed a hansom, and gave the address. Faucit sat back in the cab, smoking and thinking; Mayne leaned forward, with his arms on the doors, his face flushed with excitement and expectation.

"Suppose she is not in?" he said once. "Of course, she won't be in. She will not have had time to get home."

"Then we will wait till she is in," was the quiet reply.

After an interminable drive they reached St. Cyr Road. It was a dreary, out-of-the-way sort of place, bordered on either side by small detached villas, each surrounded by a wall the top of which was incrusted with broken glass. All were dismal, several were unoccupied. Before one of the latter the hansom stopped, and the driver lifted the trap.

"This is Alma Cottage, sir," he said, "but there don't seem to be anyone living there."

Mayne sprang out.

The name was clearly painted on each of the dingy *stuccoed* gateposts. The gate was padlocked, the garden neglected. The shutters were closed, and the blinds drawn down.

There was a bell at the gate, and the artist pulled it vigorously. It was very stiff, and beyond the creaking of the wire elicited no response.

"Perhaps there is another house of the same name," Faucit suggested to the man; "drive up the road and back, slowly."

The cabby obeyed. He walked his horse along by the kerb, scanning the names on every gate. There was no other Alma Cottage.

Mayne was still struggling with the bell. An old man, carrying an armful of gardener's tools, had stopped to look at him.

"There ain't no manner of use your ringing there, sir," he said presently; "the place has been empty this three year."

"Who does it belong to?" asked Faucit, who had come up in time to hear the last sentence.

"I've heard tell as the last party who had it was called Johnson, but I never seed anyone but the servant there. The gen'elman only came down irreg'lar like—of a night," and he grinned significantly.

"Is the place to let?"

"There's never been no board up; but Mr. Standing, the agent, used to have the letting of it."

"Where is he to be found?"

The man told him. Faucit gave him a shilling and got into the cab. "We will see the agent," he said.

The agent proved to be an affable gentleman who wore a checked suit, a crimson tie, and several rings.

Yes, he had the management of the St. Cyr Road property; knew Alma Cottage perfectly, but it was not to let. The present owner was abroad. Yes, he had been abroad for some time; but he had no intention of letting the house; had refused several offers for it already.

"I have rather a fancy for the place," Faucit suggested mendaciously; "I should be quite willing to meet your client on his own terms."

'Not the least use, sir; Mr. Johnson won't let at any price. He may return to England someday soon, and he would require the house again."

"It must get very damp," said Mayne, thoughtfully; "but I suppose there is a caretaker who looks after it."

The agent did not know.

There was nothing for it but to return to town. When Faucit had left his friend at the club he took a fresh cab, drove to a large house in Park Lane, and inquired for Mr. McCandlish. The servant informed him that his master had left for the Continent two hours before. Did not know when he would be back. The journey was quite unexpected. Mr. McCandlish had left no address; he would wire in the morning where his letters were to be sent.

Faucit gave the man his card.

"I wished particularly to see Mr. McCandlish," he said; "but I suppose I must wait now. Let me have his address as soon as you know it."

He slipped half a sovereign into the servant's hand, and went back to the club.

On the way he stopped at a telegraph office, and despatched a message:

Alma Cottage, St. Cyr Road, Hampstead. Find out all possible about owner and caretaker, if practicable to get into house. Urgent. Faucit.

The telegram was sent to Hayward, 112, Denbigh Street, Pimlico.

"One thing is certain," he said later on to Mayne, "and that is that McCandlish knows something about the girl. He saw the likeness, and he recognised the original. He was awfully upset, and he bolts forthwith. If she is alive, he is afraid of meeting her, and—"

"*If* she is alive," interrupted the artist, "why, we saw her this afternoon."

"Three of us saw her"—Faucit struck a match very deliberately—"or *thought* we did."

"I did see her," said Mayne, doggedly.

"But Bignold and Vernon did not. Why did she give you that address?"

"I don't know"—very unwillingly.

"I do. It was because that house was the last address she had to give, and I believe that it is there we shall find her."

"You think it possible that she can be concealed about the premises?"

"Yes," said Faucit, coolly.

Four days later Mayne received an urgent summons to his friend's chambers. He found him closeted with a short, commonplace man, whom he introduced as Mr. Hayward. The artist recognised the name as that of a detective whom Faucit had come across professionally, and of whose judgment and tact he held a very high opinion.

"Another link in the chain," he remarked, without wasting time in preliminaries. "Now, Hayward, tell your own story."

"Not much of a story yet, sir; but Mr. Johnson, the owner of Alma Cottage, is really McCandlish the millionaire. He took the house on lease from February '86 and put in a housekeeper. He was never there in the daytime; used to go down late at night with a friend, not always the same, and leave in a few hours or early next morning. In April '87 he bought the place, and has never occupied it since. A caretaker goes in and opens the windows now and again. Crusty old party, of the name of Short. Not to be bought; says her orders are to admit no one, and she ain't going to lose a good job along of strangers."

"What is there at the back?"

"Garden of house in Randolph Street unoccupied. Windows of adjoining houses don't overlook the premises, leastways only the garden."

Mayne rose suddenly.

"I am going over that house tonight," he said, in a hard, strained voice.

"Yes," agreed Faucit, quietly. "Will you bring some tools, Hayward?"

"It is a criminal offence, Mr. Faucit."

"I have already told you that I take the entire responsibility. You shall lose nothing by the business. What time?"

"About eleven," answered the detective, shrugging his shoulders. "Better meet me at the end of the Hampstead Road. Can't go up in hansoms, you know, sir."

At half an hour to midnight the three men reached the gate of the empty house. They had taken the precaution of separating *en route*, Faucit and Mayne keeping together, the detective following on the opposite side of the street.

The road was absolutely deserted. The inhabitants were apparently early people, and all the houses were dark. By the light of the last lamp Hayward consulted his watch. "Half-past," he said. "Constable won't pass till 11.50, we have twenty minutes to do it." He took off his coat, folded it, and threw it over the broken glass on the wall.

"I'll give you a leg up, Mr. Faucit. Drop carefully, there are bushes on the other side."

Faucit clambered over and the others followed.

Guided by the detective, they made their way round to the back. Once down the area, Hayward showed a light. Slipping a knife up the shutter of the kitchen window, he worked open the bolt, broke a pane of glass, turned the fastener, and raised the sash. They made a careful inspection of the house. Dust lay thick on the covered furniture and carpetless floors.

From room to room their footsteps echoed noisily in the dead stillness of the night. They began at the garrets and worked their way back to the basement, without finding the smallest trace of any human being, living or dead.

When they reached the door of the kitchen, Mayne's face was very pale. There were black circles round his eyes. His expression was one of utter despondency.

"We'd better go, gentlemen," said Hayward; "there is nothing more to be seen, I think."

He held up the lantern and looked round.

"Wait a bit," he added. "There is a cellar."

A stout oak door opened from the darkest corner of the passage. It was secured by a couple of heavy bolts, and across the lock was drawn a tape fastened by two seals.

"Wine-cellar," suggested Faucit.

He slid the bolts, which were rusty and moved with difficulty.

Hayward took a small bag from his pocket, and proceeded scientifically to pick the lock. In five minutes, they were standing inside. It was a wine-cellar, fitted with bins, most of which were empty. There were a few bottles of champagne and half a dozen or so of spirits.

"Not enough stuff to justify all that precaution," remarked Faucit.

The detective stooped, holding the lantern close to the ground.

"Bricks loose here," he said. "This floor has been taken up and never properly relaid."

He knelt down, sifting the dust and little bits of loose mortar in his fingers. Presently he drew out what looked like a dustweb, and held it carefully to the light, gently disengaging the clinging particles and smoothing it between his thumb and forefinger. It was a long, silky hair.

"Look here, sir" he said, "here's a clue at last. There's a light poker in the kitchen that will serve our turn. Just you wait a minute till I fetch it."

Faucit laid his hand on Mayne's arm, and felt in the darkness that he was shaking from head to foot.

Hayward was back in a second. He slipped the thin end of the poker between the bricks, using it as a lever. Very little effort dislodged them. When he had removed a dozen, he thrust his arm into the hole, scraping up handfuls of rubbish and loose earth. Each handful he examined by the light of the lantern. The upper layer was chiefly brick-dust and earth. Lower down the dust was largely mixed with a white substance.

"Quicklime," ejaculated the detective. "I should not wonder, Mr. Faucit, if you weren't right after all."

He lengthened the aperture, working with a will, till the bricks were removed for a space of nearly six feet. Then he and Faucit scraped up the earth.

Two feet below the surface they come upon a complete bed of lime.

"Gently," said Hayward; "we've come to what we are looking for."

Taking out his handkerchief, he carefully swept away the white dust.

The two men bent forward, with a sickening instinct of what lay beneath that thin covering. Suddenly the detective looked up.

"Mr. Faucit," he remarked, quietly, "just see to your friend. He'll be off in a second."

The warning was not a minute too soon. Before the words were fairly past his lips, Mayne had reeled and pitched heavily into Faucit's arms, in a dead faint.

As he caught the unconscious man, the barrister looked down into the cavity and saw lying at his very feet—*the perfect skeleton of a woman.*

It was all that remained of the most beautiful model in London—the girl whose fate had for three years been wrapped in mystery—the original of Deverill's "Œnone," Violet Lucas.

A Ghost's Revenge

It was a dismal evening. Heavy clouds covered the sky. The air was full of a raw dampness, which hung like a veil over the flat marshy district through which the London train was winding its way, like some huge fiery serpent, now pausing in its sinuous course, now darting forward with a writhe and a shriek, to vanish under a lurid cloud of steam.

"Mallowby," shouted the hoarse voice of the porter, "Mallowby." The door of a first-class smoking carriage was reluctantly opened, and a solitary passenger alighted.

"What a beast of a night!" he muttered, hastily buttoning up his fur-lined overcoat, "and what a beast of a place!" peering discontentedly across the low white railing at the monotonous stretch of snow-powdered fallow and pasture. "What on earth has induced Forster to bury himself in such a desolate hole?"

"Any luggage, sir? Two portmanteaus and a guncase—very good, sir. Where for—the Rectory? The cart is just outside, through the gate on the left."

With another malediction on the rawness of the atmosphere, the passenger from town picked his way across the sloppy platform and climbed into the dogcart which was in waiting for him. He was cold, hungry, and, if the truth must be told, considerably out of temper; and, as he splashed down the mile of muddy road which lay between the station and the village, Gerald Harrison was half inclined to repent his promise of spending a couple of days with his old college chum on his way to Scotland.

A hearty welcome, a sherry and bitters, a roaring fire, and a hot bath went a long way towards dispelling his ill-humour. The Reverend Richard Forster, now acting as *locum tenens* for the absent rector of Mallowby, thoroughly understood the art of making his guests comfortable.

"You will not have too much time, old fellow," he said, when he had conducted Harrison to his room. "I am sorry to hurry you, but dinner is at half-past seven, and I cannot well put it back because I have asked another man. His name is Granville. He has lately come to the old Hall, and we are going to shoot over one of his farms tomorrow."

Twenty minutes later, when Gerald (with temperature and temper alike restored to their normal condition) descended to the library, he found his host in earnest confabulation with the visitor—a slight dark man, with an anxious, rather worried expression, and a trick of glancing nervously over his shoulder.

"I give you my word, Forster," he was saying, "that it is going on worse than ever. I can't get a servant to sleep in the front of the house, and if I were not ashamed of acknowledging myself a fool, I would cut the place tomorrow and go back to town."

The opening of the door put an end to the discussion. Forster changed the subject by introducing his guests, and as dinner was almost immediately announced, the conversation fell into general channels—such as the Irish question, pheasant-rearing, and the chances of an open season. It struck Harrison that Mr. Granville had all the appearance of a man who has received some severe mental shock. Though he talked intelligently and even well, it was evident that his attention was never wholly given to the subject in hand. He seemed to be constantly listening for some expected sound, and once, when footsteps were audible on the gravel without, he started violently and turned as white as a sheet.

"It is only Kenwell bringing back the keys of the church," remarked Forster. "He has been taking the choir practice for me this evening. There is the bell."

A servant answered the door, and the footsteps died away again, accompanied by the distant clash of the iron gate. Granville sank back in his chair with a long breath of relief. He had let his cigar out, and now looked round for a light. Harrison offered him a match, and, as the elder man took it, he could feel that his hand was cold and shaking.

The evening passed in pleasant desultory chat. At eleven o'clock Granville rose. "Will you order my cart?" he said. Then, in answer to his host's demur, he answered nervously, "Don't tempt me to stay, Forster; it only makes matters worse. Yes, I know it is quite early and all that; but they will take ten minutes to put the horse in, and," with a ghastly attempt at a smile, "I am like Cinderella, I must be indoors before midnight. You will come up early tomorrow, and of course you both lunch with me. I would ask you to dine as well, only—only I am not good company in my own house now."

Forster's hand was on the bell. He paused, and looked keenly into his friend's face.

"Don't go back, Granville," he said, earnestly. "Let me tell your man that you will stay the night here. I can easily put you up."

"No, thanks; no," with the nervous haste of one who fears that his resolution may fail him, "I cannot do that. After all I have said, I dare not show the white feather to the servants. They would think me a fool; but, my God! they don't hear it as I do. Tell them to bring the cart round, Forster. For pity's sake, man, don't waste time! It is ten minutes past eleven already."

The order was given. As the minutes wore on, Granville became increasingly uneasy. He could not restrain his restless anxiety to be off, and it was a relief to every one when the grating of wheels outside announced that the trap was in readiness. Forster accompanied him to the door, whither Harrison presently followed.

"It is not much of a night," he commented, peering out into the chill darkness. "Your friend will have a coolish drive."

Forster was standing on the step.

"Hush!" he said, holding up his hand. "Listen! He is galloping."

From the old grey tower on their left chimed the half-hour, and, as the notes died away, they could hear the receding rattle of a cart being driven at a furious pace along the road below.

"He must be cracked to drive at that rate in the dark," cried Gerald, as the clatter of hoofs grew fainter and finally died away. "It will be more by luck than management if he doesn't upset at the first corner. What is the matter with him, Dick—does he drink, or is he off his head?"

"Neither at present. He thinks his house is haunted, and it is getting on his nerves."

"Oh, he must be cracked, then," with easy decision.

"No one but a lunatic believes in ghosts in these days. Accept the possibilities of terrestrial elementaries and left-hand magic if you like; but the common or garden ghost, never."

"There is something queer about the old Hall, though," persisted Forster. "I do not believe that any consideration you could offer would induce a Mallowby man to sleep there alone. The place has a bad name. It stood empty for years before Granville bought it. He spent no end of money in repairs and furniture too, which makes it additionally hard on him to be driven out by—"

"A ghost," concluded Harrison, with a shout of laughter. "My dear Dick, it is too absurd. Let us exorcise the place. I will back my six-shooter at thirty feet against any combination of goblins and blue fire. We will arrange a match tomorrow. Fifty pounds a side, to be paid in material currency only. Come, admit now that the thing is a huge joke."

"It is a good deal more like death to Granville," returned Forster, seriously. "His nerves are regularly gone to pieces. He is not like the same fellow who came down in the autumn."

"Have the ghosts been trying to evict him ever since?

"Sounds weak, I dare say," Dick answered, "but I am inclined to believe, Gerald, that there is more in it than meets the eye. Last October Granville was every bit as sceptical as you are. If he heard anything, he treated it with contempt. When the servants complained of mysterious noises, he laughed them to scorn. You saw for yourself that he does not laugh at it now. He told me this evening that these—these—manifestations are of nightly occurrence. I am afraid it is taking serious effect upon his health. I wish I had kept him here tonight."

"Oh, he will be all right," said Harrison, lightly. "Funk is a deuced unpleasant complaint, but it don't often kill. Twelve o'clock; I think I'll be turning in. This time tomorrow, I suppose, we shall be wishing each other a happy new year."

But the glad new year was destined to be ushered in by no hearty shaking of hands, no joyous congratulations at Mallowby Rectory. In the grey dawn of the December morning Harrison was awakened by the flashing of a candle before his eyes. Forster was standing beside the bed, with a pale and horror-stricken face.

"Gerald," he said hurriedly, "will you get up at once? I want you to come with me to the Hall. Something terrible has happened. Poor Granville is dead."

"Dead!" repeated the other blankly, "dead! Why, he only left here at eleven."

"I know that. Seven hours ago he was here, only seven hours ago, and now they are carrying his body up from the pond where it was found. Why did I not keep him?" he cried, pacing the room in deep agitation. "Why did I let him go back to that accursed house? I knew his mind was unhinged by what he had heard there. Poor fellow! poor Granville! and now it is too late."

Harrison was already out of bed, "I will be downstairs in five minutes," he said. "Of course, I know no particulars, but has anyone thought of sending for a doctor?"

Forster caught eagerly at the implied hope.

"Someone shall go for Mr. Tilling at once," he said, hurrying out of the room.

It was a relief to be able to do something, but long before the surgeon arrived, they knew that his services would be useless. Death had sealed the master of Ravenshill for his own. The cold and rigid limbs refused to respond to the revivifying influences of hot blankets and artificial respiration.

Harrison was of opinion, as he assisted in his friend's frantic endeavours to restore some semblance of life, that poor Granville had been dead for several hours.

It was a painful task. In vain Forster tried to close the dull, lacklustre eyes, fixed in a wide stare of indescribable horror. The tense features would not relax. Never had human being passed away from life leaving behind him so terrible an impression of fear. At seven o'clock the surgeon for whom Forster had sent appeared on the scene. One glance at the body was sufficient for him.

"He's dead," said the plain-spoken country practitioner. "Dead as a door-nail. How did it happen?"

Ah! how indeed? That was a mystery. A secret known only to the dead man and to those unspeakable powers who work behind the veil.

In the early morning of the last day of the year the household at the Hall had been startled from their slumbers by a wild, agonised cry, followed by shriek upon shriek of demoniacal laughter. The horrible sounds lasted only for a minute. Before the terrified servants were fairly aroused and crowding together into the corridor, to learn the meaning of this strange alarm, the house was wrapped in its customary silence. For a few moments they had been too scared to do more than wonder at their master remaining undisturbed; then someone, bolder than the rest, suggested that it would be as well to waken him. They knocked at his door and received no answer. They called, but no voice replied.

At last the butler ventured into the room. It was empty. The night lamp, which Granville had lately used, was burning brightly, the fire was nearly out. The bed had not been occupied. Thoroughly alarmed now, a search party was formed, and, armed with lights and a brace of revolvers, the men descended to the ground floor. In the library the lamp was also burning. The odour of tobacco still hung in the air; a few embers glowed in the grate; the spirit decanters and an empty soda-water bottle lay on the table beside an open book. There was no trace of any disturbance, and there was no sign of Granville.

The servants looked at each other in silence. No one dared to put into words the fear that lay chill at his heart. Suddenly the butler uttered an exclamation. His eyes had fallen on one of the windows. The long curtains were swaying gently backward and forward in the current of cold air from without.

The shutters were thrown back, and the casement stood wide open. They crowded round. "Steady, keep back a bit," protested one man, more astute than his fellows, "there is snow enough to hold footmarks. It's a pity to tread it about till we've got a lantern and struck the trail."

In a few minutes a covered light had been procured, and the threshold of the window was examined. There could be no doubt as to the way in which Granville had quitted the room. Straight from the sill the footprints were distinctly traced in the light snow. Along the path they tracked the marks, round the corner of the house, across the lawn to the edge of the pond. And there, beneath the willows, half-hidden by the drooping frost-browned ferns, they found the body of their master, still in evening dress, with clenched fingers, and features transfixed in an expression of ghastly dread.

The quiet little village was shaken to its core. All day long the people gathered in knots to discuss the awful tragedy which had been enacted in their midst. Horror was in the air. Old superstition reasserted its sway with renewed strength. Old stories were repeated with bated breath; for once again the curse of the Deverels had fallen, and the truth of the half-forgotten legend was triumphantly vindicated.

By nightfall every human being had quitted the precincts of the fateful Hall. The scared domestics absolutely refused to remain on the premises, and the big house was deserted, save for the silent form lying so still beneath the white sheet on one of the sofas in the library, in which room the body of Philip Granville had been laid to await the coroner's inquest.

To Forster this desertion of the helpless corpse seemed terrible. He would have spent the night in watching beside the poor fellow who had so lately been his guest, and was only dissuaded from his purpose by the earnest solicitations of his churchwarden, a stalwart farmer, on whose grey head seventy odd years sat lighter than most men's fifty.

"Parson," said the old man, solemnly, "theer's noa good a fly in' in the faace o' Providence. Noa body thinks as you're a coward, but what sort o' lise be theer in flingin' good loives a'ter bad uns? Yon poor lad tried it, and see how they've served him. Thirty year back Lord Broadborough's agent died in saame way. My feyther used to tell how, when he were a little lad, one of the Dawbenys caam doon hissen' and boasted as how he'd better the Deverels. It was i' the summer toime, and all went well enow. But as soon as winter caame on, 'they' were at work ag'in, and t'ould squoire, he began to grow graave and stern-like. He would na gi' in, till, on New Year's Eve, the house were fetched up by a fearful cry, and next mornin' they found his body in the pond theer, with a look on t'faace as, God forbid, should iver be sean on yours or moine.

"Mony an' mony a good mon has met that death, sin' the noight that Katharine Deverel stood in yon winder and cursed the mon who had robbed her of her husband's naame, an' theer lad of his lawful inheritance. 'You hev ta'an it by fraud,' she croid; 'but the Lord will avenge me. Noa good shall it bring thee. You shall neyther live in it yoursen, nor shall another receive it at your hands. Though I lose my immortal soul,' she says, 'I'll hev revenge. You may tak' my choild's birthright, you may slur ma fair naame, but noa mon—be he young or auld, good or evil, so that he does na' bear th' naame o' Deverel—shall live to see a new year dawn wi'in these walls. I'll die on Deverel land,' says she; 'and he who braves ma curse shall die even as I hev died.'

"Then she called on the God of the feytherless to hear her words and turned awa', and next mornin' they found her body stiff an' stark in yonder pond, with the dead baby still clasped in her arms. You'll bear in moind, sir, what the Lord did to the mon who built up the walls o' Jericho. It's His will, an' you bein' a parson, should knaw better than to goa agin' Him. What harm can taake yon poor bit o' clay now? But you hev a wark to do i' the warld, and you ain't got no reet to chuck you loife a'ter his'n."

"Mr. Dawson is right, Dick," urged Harrison; "you can't do the poor fellow any good. Your nerves are shaken, and I am free to confess, ghost or no ghost, to spend the night in that dismal house with a dead man is more than I should care about."

Very unwillingly Forster at last agreed to yield.

Three days later the local jury brought in a verdict of "Died by the visitation of God," and once again the spirit of Katharine Deverel had triumphed and the home of her ancestors stood empty.

★★★★★★★★

Five years had come and gone, bringing with them many changes. Dick Forster, now Bishop of Honduras, was doing good work for God and man in his far-off colonial diocese. His place in Harrison's daily life had been filled by another friend of his schoolboy days, who was also shortly to become his brother-in-law. Jack Chamberlayne was a handsome, genial young fellow, blessed with a fine constitution, a sweet temper, and a very considerable fortune, and the match between his favourite sister and his special chum was a source of unmixed satisfaction to Gerald.

The two men were constantly together until a matter of business obliged Harrison to visit the South of Europe. The transaction occupied him for some months, and it was not till the end of December that he found himself once more on English soil. He reached Dover at noon on the last day of the year, and went straight to the "Lord Warden." A packet of letters was awaiting him. They had been forwarded from San Carrémo after his departure, and among them was an envelope addressed in Chamberlayne's characteristic handwriting. The letter ran:

Dear old boy, what do you mean by spending Christmas in a dirty Italian village, instead of returning to the bosom of your family like a respectable Englishman? I don't believe a word about the vineyards. Tell your agent to go to the devil, and come to us for the new year, or neither Elaine nor I will have anything more to do with you. The Hunt Ball is on the 5th, the Cardwell's on the following evening. On the 7th Mrs. Verelst is giving some theatricals in which we are going to distinguish ourselves, and there are three or four other minor events which you ought not to miss. Also, I want your valuable advice as to the wisdom of buying a place in Creamshire. I only heard of it last week, and have already made up my mind to purchase, so your counsel must tend in that direction if you wish me to profit by it.

It is a jolly old house, with capital stabling, and nice gardens. There is a ripping tennis-lawn (room for two courts, if I fill up a pond at the end), and a lot of old oak indoors. I forgot to say the house is furnished. It is in the best part of the Broadborough country, and within reach of the outside meets of Lord Cremorne's and the Turton. Plenty of shooting, and the whole thing going for a mere song. I believe there is even a family

ghost thrown in. I am running down on Friday for a week to
see how I like it; but of course, you will put up at my place as
you come through town whether I am there or not—

Harrison waited to hear no more. In a moment the letter was
crushed into his pocket, and he was out in the street, and, hurrying
to the nearest telegraph-office, without a second's delay he wrote the
message and handed it in to the clerk—

Chamberlayne, 112 Piccadilly.—On no account go to Ravenshill Hall till you have seen me. Shall be in town this afternoon
and will explain.—Gerald.

Then he hastened back to the hotel and ordered some luncheon.
While he was eating, he looked out the trains for town. The next was
due in twenty minutes. His portmanteaus had not been unstrapped.
Harrison sent for a cab, paid his bill, and in less than an hour was well
on his way to London. From the moment of reading Chamberlayne's
description of his projected purchase, he had decided on the course
he must pursue. Though the name of the place was not mentioned he
knew, by a sudden swift intuition, that it was Ravenshill Hall. Back to
his mind, with the freshness of yesterday, swept the memory of that
terrible night five years ago, and he shuddered as he recalled the words
of the old farmer.

"No man—be he young or old, good or evil, so that he does not
bear the name of Deverel—shall live to see the new year break within
these walls. I will die on Deverel land, and he who braves my curse
shall die even as I have died."

"Many and many a good man has met that death since." Was another victim destined to be added to the long roll-call of that terrible
vengeance, and that victim his old playmate, his friend, his almost
brother? No, thank God; there was yet time to avert the stroke of fate.
Jack must have received his wire by now. He would be waiting for the
promised explanation.

The slow hours wore on; the train rattled and ground its way
through the wintry landscape. The sky was leaden and dull. On the
horizon lay dense masses of clouds, black and heavy with snow. By
the time they ran into Charing Cross, large flakes were floating lazily
down to join their crushed and mud-stained comrades on the dirty
pavement. Evidently there had been a considerable fall earlier in the
day, for the roofs down the Strand were gleaming white, and great
heaps of snow had been scraped up from the roadway and piled be-

hind the pillars of the station gates. Harrison got his luggage on to a hansom and drove straight to his friend's chambers. As he glanced up at the windows, it struck him as odd that no lights were to be seen.

The housekeeper answered his ring.

"Oh, is it you, Mr. Harrison? Very glad to see you back, sir. There is a letter for you upstairs and three telegrams. The first came on Wednesday, sir. The note Mr. Chamberlayne left for you; he expected you would be here on Wednesday."

"Left for me," repeated Gerald, anxiously. "He has not gone, surely? Did he not get my wire?"

"I sent it on with the other letters this morning, sir. Mr. Chamberlayne has been gone a week—him and Mr. Curtis. He is staying at Creamshire, at Ravenshill Hall, Mallowby."

Harrison's brain reeled. He saw it all now. That letter had been a week in travelling to Italy and back again to England. He had cried, "Peace, peace," when there was no peace; when all the time he was too late, and Jack had gone to that accursed house, and—this was New Year's Eve.

"Fetch the letters, Mrs. Williams; or, stay, I will get them myself."

He tore upstairs, two steps at a time, snatched the envelopes from the mantelpiece and was back to the cab before the astounded housekeeper could utter a syllable.

"King's Cross!" he shouted to the driver; "and a double fare if I catch the 7.5 for the north. It is a matter of life and death."

"I'll do my best, sir," said the man, dubiously; "but it's darned bad going."

Never had the way seemed so long; never did time go faster and horse more slowly. To Harrison's overwrought fancy they crept along, and again and again he raised the trap and implored the man to whip up. The agony and anxiety in his white drawn face moved the cabby's heart to pity, and he generously refrained from swearing at his impetuous fare.

"A cove is that onreasonabie when 'e's in trouble," he growled to himself aloft. "Does 'e want me to let the mare down and make sure of losing 'is blooming train?"

At last they turned into the Euston Road. The snow was coming down in good earnest now, and Gerald could hardly see the hands of the clock for the blinding flakes. It wanted eight minutes to seven.

"Thank God!" he murmured, as the hansom turned into the yard of the Great Northern. Before the man had time to pull up, he was out on the ground.

"Mallowby," he called to the porter, "can I do it?"

"Four minutes," was the response.

Gerald flung half a sovereign to the driver, and rushed into the booking-office. The bell was ringing when he got on to the platform. The porter had put his portmanteaus into a carriage and was holding open the door. He threw himself into a seat with a sense of gratitude that he was to have the compartment to himself.

To maintain an appearance of indifferent calm at this moment would, he felt, have been impossible. He was enduring a martyrdom of suspense. If his friend's life had not already paid the forfeit for another's sin, every second that ticked its course was bringing him nearer to its end. He conjured up with horrible distinctness the dark library, the deep recesses on either side of the fireplace lined with books, the massive oak furniture.

He could hear the weird murmur of voices, without, the ghostly steps on the drive; then the heavy velvet curtains trembled, parted, and a woman's figure stood framed in the long window—a woman with dripping garments and a white set face, lighted by strange, lurid eyes—eyes which were dead, and yet alive in their fierce hatred and unquenchable thirst for revenge. How they glittered! They were close to him now, looking in through the carriage window, and Harrison, who had once laughed contemptuously at the mere notion of supernatural manifestations, was perilously near raising a ghost for himself from the intensity of his nervous excitement. Fortunately, at this juncture he remembered that Jack's letter and the telegrams were still unopened in his pocket, and the break in the sequence of thought gave him time to pull himself together.

With a half-laugh at his own weakness, he drew the curtains across the windows, and, lighting a cigar, tore open the yellow envelopes.

All three messages had been handed in at Mallowby Station

The first was dated December 29, and said:

Come down as soon as possible. Dull and seedy. Want cheering up.—Chamberlayne.

"He is getting nervous," Gerald said to himself "and did not like to acknowledge it."

The second telegram was more urgent, and enclosed a reply form.

Must see you today. Important. Wire what train. Don't fail me.—Jack.

95

The third was signed by Chamberlayne's valet.

Something seriously wrong here. Please come at once, very anxious about master.

Harrison's face grew very grave. Something must indeed have been wrong before the punctilious Curtis would take upon himself to send a wire like that. His fears returned with renewed force. It was torture to think of Jack sending message after message only to meet with blank silence. There was a piteous reproach in the last appeal, "Don't fail me."

"As if I were likely to do that so long as I am above ground," thought Gerald. "Poor old Jack, he might have known I should have answered if I'd ever got the things."

At Peterborough he went to the refreshment-room and swallowed a sandwich and a few mouthfuls of soup while his flask was replenished with brandy. Very few passengers joined the train, and no one came into Harrison's carriage. As the hours dragged out their weary length, he grew more and more restless and nervous. He paced the six feet of floor like a caged animal. He let down the window. A cloud of fine snow blew in through the opening. All around hedges, fields, and trees were wrapped in a dense white mantle. It was bitterly cold. Despite his fur-lined coat, hot tin, and a couple of rugs, his teeth were chattering and his hands were like ice.

He looked at his watch. It was half-past nine. In thirty minutes, the train was due at Mallowby, and they had not passed Grantham yet. Surely, too, they were slackening speed. Half doubting the evidence of his senses, he again opened the window. The train was unmistakably at a standstill, but there was not the slightest sign of a station. The wind had risen, and whistled through the telegraph-wires overhead. Between the gusts he could hear the murmur of voices. Presently a man passed along the footboard. It was the guard. Harrison inquired the cause of the delay.

"Line blocked, I'm afraid, sir," was the reply, "but I will let you know as I come back."

With an exclamation, which was almost a groan, Gerald flung himself back in his seat. Were the fates league against him, that now, when every moment might seal Jack Chamberlayne's death-warrant, he must perforce sit idle, bound hand and foot by the victory of the forces of nature over the inventions of man? Five minutes passed, ten, twenty, thirty. Then the guard put his head in at the door.

"All right, sir, line is clear; we shall go on directly."

At one minute past eleven the London train, more than an hour behind its time, set down a single passenger at Mallowby. Harrison at once addressed himself to the station master, and inquired how he could get to the old Hall. The man had been on the coroner's jury five years before, and remembered his face.

"Going to the Hall tonight, sir? Why, were not you here when poor Mr. Granville was drowned? You don't want to see it a second time, surely!"

"God forbid!" answered Gerald, quickly, "but I want to prevent it. A dear friend of mine is at that devilish house tonight. He does not know his danger, and I mean to save him."

"You can't do it," returned the man, bluntly. "Best keep clear of the black work that will be going forward up there. There is no baulking the Deverel curse. It will have its victim God help him I say, and all those who sleep under that roof on New Year's Eve. You can do nothing for them."

"I mean to try," answered Harrison, with set teeth. "I have no time to waste. Where can I get a trap?"

"Nowhere nearer than the village. It will take you as long as walking the whole way. The roads are awful."

"Then I must walk. Can you find me a lantern? For Heaven's sake be quick. Every minute may mean his life now. What do I care about the danger? Man, I tell you he is my friend. He is to marry my sister in a fortnight, and I will either save him or die with him."

The stationmaster hesitated a moment.

"Look here, sir," he said, hurriedly, "you're a brave man, and I'll do what I can to help you. That was my last train till 1.30. I'll come with you as far as the gates. It will save you losing the way, and perhaps a bit of time getting through the drifts beside."

Gerald thanked him heartily, and side by side they turned their backs to the lights of the little station, and struck into the lonely road which lay between the railway and the haunted house. It had ceased snowing now. A few stars gleamed out between the rifts in the cloudy sky. From time to time a pale moon showed her face, now flooding the white landscape with a cold grey light, now hiding herself in a veil of fleecy vapour, as though she feared to see those things which should be done on the earth. By the help of the stationmaster's lantern the two men managed to keep to the narrow cart tract.

The road was desperately bad. In places the snow was fully two feet deep. With the rising moon a keen wind had got up, which came sweeping over the level fields right in their faces, and cut like a knife. At the turning into the village where the land sloped a little, the drifts were almost impassable. At every step they sank above the knee. Harrison could hear his companion's breath coming thick and short. He was evidently getting done. For himself he was impervious to all outward discomfort. Cold, fatigue, hunger; he was vaguely conscious that he should know them all, if he were not past feeling now. His whole mind, will, nerve, aye, his very being, were centred in the one intense determination to save his friend.

At length they gained the main street of the village. Here the snow was trodden down, and the going comparatively easy. Hardly a light was to be seen in any of the cottages. Involuntarily Gerald's eyes turned towards the rectory. It was wrapped in shadow and silence; but from the old grey tower, looming up behind, gleamed a small point of yellow light. Slowly it crept from window to window, steadily rising, rising. A cold shudder ran through the man who watched it. He knew what it meant; that the last sands were falling from the hour-glass of time; that the life of the old year must now be measured by minutes. The ringers were going up to the belfry.

"Oh, God! "he groaned inwardly, "give me strength, give me time."

"Have you got a drop of brandy about you, sir?" suggested the practical Miles. "It would help to keep the spirit in us a bit."

Without slackening his pace, Gerald held cut his flask.

"A'ter you, sir, a'ter you."

"I don't want any, thanks." His ears were strained for the first stroke of that ominous bell.

"Oh, come now, sir, fair do's. You will need your strength more than me, and I say a'ter you."

To save discussion, Harrison put the flask to his lips. The spirit sent a warm glow through his sluggish veins. At the same moment the stillness of the night was broken by the solemn tolling of the passing bell. With a cry of horror, he thrust the brandy into his companion's hands, and began to run as if for his life. Immediately before him the road curved sharply to the left, and far ahead through the skeleton branches of the leafless elms gleamed half a dozen irregular patches of light. They shone from the windows of the Hall.

Slowly, mournfully pealed the muffled notes from the belfry. The knell of the old year, dying hard in the chill winter night; the knell of a human soul, who might even now be passing from life and love to the horror of unknown darkness, through the gate of a fearful death. The thought was torture. How he lived through those moments of suspense Harrison never knew. He could not have told how he covered the ground, or when he passed the gates which led up to the house. His brain burned like molten iron, on which the slow, monotonous clang of the bell fell like the strokes of a heavy hammer.

He forgot the stationmaster, plodding along in the rear—forgot everything but that his goal was reached, if only he had not come too late.

The lower windows were closed, but from the chinks in the shutters stole the warm glow of fire and lamp, and as he reached the corner of the house, he could catch the sound of approaching voices. Voices, yes!—but what sort of voices? Nearer they came, now swelling louder, now sinking to a whisper, but ever drawing nearer, till he could hear the words repeated in every shade of tone, from malignant exultation to concentrated passion of resolve.

"We shall have him tonight!" they said, with ghastly reiteration. "We shall have him tonight!"

Like a wave of ice-cold air, the horrible sounds passed by him, receded, and died away with an echo of fiendish laughter.

Despite, an inexpressible thrill of fear, that sent a shudder through his whole frame and nearly raised the hair on his head, Harrison was conscious of a faint hope that all was not over yet. Slowly and more slowly came the tolling of the bell. It was on the verge of midnight.

Suddenly from within the closed windows of the library issued a wild awful cry. The shutters were flung back, as if by magic the casement was thrown open, and the dark shadow of a man crossed the sill.

The moon emerging suddenly from behind a bank of clouds poured down a flood of silvery light on the stone wall, the snow-covered path, and on the figure of Jack Chamberlayne, who, with hands clenched as if in mortal pain, his eyes fixed with an expression of nameless horror on some object, invisible to all but him, was slowly following the ghostly vision along the drive, across the lawn, to—

With a supreme effort Harrison threw off the paralysing numbness which was creeping over him. Instinctively he dashed across the grass and stood between Chamberlayne and the fatal pond. Twelve paces from him his friend was advancing, slowly, unswervingly, like one who walks in his sleep.

"Jack," he shouted, "Jack, it is I, Gerald. Don't you know me?"

There was not a quiver of the tense eyeballs, not a sign that his voice had reached those ears, deaf now to all earthly sounds, but from the open window of the library a man rushed towards them, crying wildly, "Stop him, for God's sake, stop him before it is too late."

Gathering all his strength, Gerald flung himself upon the approaching figure. A frantic struggle ensued, for Chamberlayne was the taller by a head, and was at this moment, moreover, endowed with abnormal strength. It was then that his knowledge of wrestling, acquired during a "long" spent in the Cumberland dales, stood Harrison in right good stead. He closed with his antagonist, and by a sudden dexterous manoeuvre threw him heavily to the ground, while overhead across the snowy fields the bells rang out their joyous welcome to the glad new year.

"Is he—dead?"

The valet on his knees beside his master's prostrate form had torn open Chamberlayne's vest and shirt, and was feeling for the faint pulsation which tells that the spirit has not yet quitted its earthly tenement.

"Fainted, I think; I can feel his heart beat."

"Thank God, sir, you came when you did. I should have been too late. Can you help me to carry him, Mr. Harrison? No, not to that d——d place!" as Gerald glanced involuntarily towards the lighted windows. "They are all up at the gardener's cottage. I wanted Mr. Chamberlayne to sleep there tonight; but you know what he is—told me go myself if I was frightened. I had not been out of the room five minutes when I heard that awful cry, and—Holy Virgin! What is that?"

Harrison turned instinctively towards the library window. From the open sash a long tongue of yellow flame leaped out, curling round the edge of the curtain and licking up the thick silk cording as though it were a mere thread. Then another, and another. Fanned by the fresh breeze from without, the yellow glare broadened and deepened till the whole room was filled with a fierce lurid glow, succeeded by dense clouds of smoke and an ominous crackling sound.

"The place is on fire!" cried Gerald. "There is not a moment to lose. We must get your master into shelter and give the alarm!"

"Holy St. Patrick, defend us!" murmured Curtis, hastily crossing himself, as he stooped to raise the helpless form of poor Chamberlayne. Then, as best they could, the two men carried their burden across the lawn, along the drive, and up the side path leading to the fruit-gardens.

"Who is in the house?" gasped Harrison, as, staggering and breathless, they reached the door of the cottage. "Are any servants there?"

"Not a soul. Mrs. Bamfield here came in the day. She left directly dinner was served. There is no one in the place to burn but the devil's spawn as lighted it"

The valet's resonant knocks soon brought the gardener to the door, and while his wife was helping Curtis to restore his master to consciousness, Bamfield hurried Gerald off to the village to obtain assistance.

Just outside the gates they encountered the station-master, who was hanging about in great distress of mind, too anxious on Harrison's account to return to Mallowby, yet not daring to adventure himself within the fatal precincts of the Hall. His relief and joy at finding Gerald still alive knew no bounds, and he readily undertook to see a messenger despatched for the nearest doctor on his way back to the station. Meanwhile an alarm had been raised, and the sleeping village was raised by the hoarse cries of "Fire!" The ringers had been the first to see the red glare through the trees; but before long some forty men had turned out to join the little crowd already assembled before the burning house.

Under Harrison's direction a body of labourers, headed by the gardener and bailiff, made an attempt to check the progress of the flames. But their efforts were scarcely perceptible. With a sharp wind blowing, and no better appliances at command than a line of buckets and a couple of garden-hose, it was evident from the first that the Hall was practically doomed. The old oak, of which the interior was chiefly built, burned like tinder. Within twenty minutes of the first outbreak the flames had spread to the upper story. Window after window lent its aid to that weird illumination. The great carved bedsteads, the massive presses and cabinets glowed and crackled in the fierce heat.

Deverel after Deverel, clothed in dainty satin or shining armour, shrivelled and cracked away from their frames, to go down calm and unflinching as became true knights and brave gentlewomen into that burning fiery furnace. Still the fire-fiend raged on, vast clouds of black smoke mingling with the glare, while from time to time could be heard the heavy crash of falling beams and flooring. As the clock of the old church chimed the first hour of the new year, with a sound like the roll of distant artillery, swelling gradually into a deafening roar, the roof fell in and there shot up to heaven one mighty sheet of flame, which turned the sky into a crimson pall, and lighted up the snow-clad country for miles around.

Was it a trick of over-heated imagination, a play of superstitious fancy, or did those who stood by at that moment really hear that hideous peal of shrill triumphant laughter, which made the stoutest heart among them quail, and forced each man to edge involuntarily nearer his neighbour? It lasted but for an instant, then nothing was audible but the continuous roar of the flames. Before the pale dawn had warmed into the red flush of sunrise, Ravenshill Hall was a heap of smouldering ashes enclosed in four grim, smoke-blackened walls. From attic to cellar not a corner had been spared. The fire had done its work thoroughly, and of the original structure nothing remained save the bare tottering shell.

"It wer' th' Lord's will," said old Dawson, who had come down to inspect the scene of the late catastrophe, "that Katharine Deverel should hev her reets; and now as He's proved as mon caan't go agin' Him, He's maade awa' wi' th' dommed ould plaace, an' a good riddance too. The Lord avenges the widder and the feytherless, though He keeps 'un waitin' a bit first soomtoimes, and it seams to me," concluded the farmer, thoughtfully, "as soom o' they poor bodies in Oireland should be hevin' theer turn afore long."

"It will be a bad lookout for the Moonlighters when they do," answered Harrison, with a quiet smile.

He was a little oppressed by the situation in which he found himself; for the events of that New Year's Eve were the talk of the countryside, and Gerald the hero of the hour. A man who, single-handed, had braved the Deverel ghosts and baulked them of their prey ranked, by the Mallowby standard, above Gordon, and only a little lower than Nelson. The worthy Miles was never tired of recounting the incidents of that midnight walk, and drew upon his imagination for certain effective touches to that part of the adventure to which he had not been an eyewitness.

The rustic mind is slow to receive a new impression; but when it does get a sensation, it makes the most of it. The people would listen to the story twenty times a day. They repeated it to each other; they turned it inside and out and discussed it threadbare, beginning it over again for the benefit of every fresh comer. To Gerald, who was heartily sick of the place and the subject, this lionising was inexpressibly irritating, and he was thankful when the doctor at last gave permission for Chamberlayne to be removed.

Thanks to his splendid constitution, backed up by the devoted nursing of Curtis and his friend, Jack escaped brain fever; but he had received a terrible shock, and his nerves were sorely shaken. It was not till the snow-wreaths had melted on the Creamshire Wolds, and crocuses were showing their gold and purple heads above the dark earth in suburban gardens, that Harrison was called upon to officiate as best man at a very pretty wedding in a certain fashionable London church, after which ceremony Mr. and Mrs. Jack Chamberlayne went off to the Riviera, where it was hoped that southern sunshine and a little judicious excitement at Monte Carlo would efface from the bridegroom's memory the experiences of that terrible New Year's Eve.

Of what he had actually seen and heard in the awful interval between his servant's departure and his subsequent return to consciousness Chamberlayne never speaks. "I used to wonder," he once said to Gerald, "why Lazarus and those other fellows who were raised from the dead never told what they did and how they felt. I think I understand now. It was too terrible. They could not put it into words, and that is how I feel about that night—as if I had been brought back from the dead."

The Blue Room

It happened twice in my time. It will never happen again, they say, since Miss Erristoun (Mrs. Arthur, that is now,) and Mr. Calder-Maxwell between them found out the secret of the haunted room, and laid the ghost; for ghost it was, though at the time Mr. Maxwell gave it another name, Latin, I fancy, but all I can remember about it now is that it somehow reminded me of poultry-rearing. I am the housekeeper at Mertoun Towers, as my aunt was before me, and her aunt before her, and first of all my great-grandmother, who was a distant cousin of the Laird, and had married the chaplain, but being left penniless at her husband's death, was thankful to accept the post which has ever since been occupied by one of her descendants. It gives us a sort of standing with the servants, being, as it were, related to the family; and Sir Archibald and my lady have always acknowledged the connection, and treated us with more freedom than would be accorded to ordinary dependants.

Mertoun has been my home from the time I was eighteen. Something occurred then of which, since it has nothing to do with this story, I need only say that it wiped out for ever any idea of marriage on my part, and I came to the Towers to be trained under my aunt's vigilant eye for the duties in which I was one day to succeed her.

Of course, I knew there was a story about the blue tapestry room. Everyone knew that, though the old laird had given strict orders that the subject should not be discussed among the servants, and always discouraged any allusion to it on the part of his family and guests. But there is a strange fascination about everything connected with the supernatural, and orders or no orders, people, whether gentle or simple, will try to gratify their curiosity; so a good deal of surreptitious talk went on both in the drawing-room and the servants' hall, and hardly a guest came to the house but would pay a visit to the Blue Room and ask all manner of questions about the ghost.

The odd part of the business was that no one knew what the ghost was supposed to be, or even if there were any ghost at all. I tried hard to get my aunt to tell me some details of the legend, but she always reminded me of Sir Archibald's orders, and added that the tale most likely started with the superstitious fancy of people who lived long ago and were very ignorant, because a certain Lady Barbara Mertoun had died in that room.

I reminded her that people must have died, at some time or other, in pretty nearly every room in the house, and no one had thought of calling them haunted, or hinting that it was unsafe to sleep there.

She answered that Sir Archibald himself had used the Blue Room, and one or two other gentlemen, who had passed the night there for a wager, and they had neither seen nor heard anything unusual. For her part, she added, she did not hold with people wasting their time thinking of such folly, when they had much better be giving their minds to their proper business.

Somehow her professions of incredulity did not ring true, and I wasn't satisfied, though I gave up asking questions. But if I said nothing, I thought the more, and often when my duties took me to the Blue Room I would wonder why, if nothing had happened there, and there was no real mystery, the room was never used; it had not even a mattress on the fine carved bedstead, which was only covered by a sheet to keep it from the dust. And then I would steal into the portrait gallery to look at the great picture of the Lady Barbara, who had died in the full bloom of her youth, no one knew why, for she was just found one morning stiff and cold, stretched across that fine bed under the blue tapestried canopy.

She must have been a beautiful woman, with her great black eyes and splendid auburn hair, though I doubt her beauty was all on the outside, for she had belonged to the gayest set of the court, which was none too respectable in those days, if half the tales one hears of it are true; and indeed a modest lady would hardly have been painted in such a dress, all slipping off her shoulders, and so thin that one can see right through the stuff. There must have been something queer about her too, for they do say her father-in-law, who was known as the wicked Lord Mertoun, would not have her buried with the rest of the family; but that might have been his spite, because he was angry that she had no child, and her husband, who was but a sickly sort of man, dying of consumption but a month later, there was no direct heir; so that with the old lord the title became extinct, and the estates passed to the Protestant branch of the family, of which the present Sir Archibald Mertoun is the head.

Be that as it may, Lady Barbara lies by herself in the churchyard, near the lych-gate, under a grand marble tomb indeed, but all alone, while her husband's coffin has its place beside those of his brothers who died before him, among their ancestors and descendants in the great vault under the chancel.

I often used to think about her, and wonder why she died, and how; and then It happened and the mystery grew deeper than ever.

There was a family-gathering that Christmas, I remember, the first Christmas for many years that had been kept at Mertoun, and we had been very busy arranging the rooms for the different guests, for on New Year's Eve there was a ball in the neighbourhood, to which Lady Mertoun was taking a large party, and for that night, at least, the house was as full as it would hold.

I was in the linen-room, helping to sort the sheets and pillow-covers for the different beds, when my lady came in with an open letter in her hand.

She began to talk to my aunt in a low voice, explaining something which seemed to have put her out, for when I returned from carrying a pile of linen to the head-housemaid, I heard her say: "It is too annoying to upset all one's arrangements at the last moment. Why couldn't she have left the girl at home and brought another maid, who could be squeezed in somewhere without any trouble?"

I gathered that one of the visitors. Lady Grayburn, had written that she was bringing her companion, and as she had left her maid, who was ill, at home, she wanted the young lady to have a bedroom adjoining hers, so that she might be at hand to give any help that was required. The request seemed a trifling matter enough in itself, but it just so happened that there really was no room at liberty. Every bed-room on the first corridor was occupied, with the exception of the Blue Room, which, as ill-luck would have it, chanced to be next to that arranged for Lady Grayburn.

My aunt made several suggestions, but none of them seemed quite practicable, and at last my lady broke out: "Well, it cannot be helped; you must put Miss Wood in the Blue Room. It is only for one night, and she won't know anything about that silly story."

"Oh, my lady!" my aunt cried, and I knew by her tone that she had not spoken the truth when she professed to think so lightly of the ghost.

"I can't help it," her ladyship answered: "beside I don't believe there is anything really wrong with the room. Sir Archibald has slept there, and he found no cause for complaint."

"But a woman, a young woman," my aunt urged; "indeed I wouldn't run such a risk, my lady; let me put one of the gentlemen in there, and Miss Wood can have the first room in the west corridor."

"And what use would she be to Lady Grayburn out there?" said her ladyship. "Don't be foolish, my good Marris. Unlock the door between the two rooms; Miss Wood can leave it open if she feels nervous; but I shall not say a word about that foolish superstition, and I shall be very much annoyed if anyone else does so."

She spoke as if that settled the question, but my aunt wasn't easy. "The laird," she murmured; "what will he say to a lady being put to sleep there?"

"Sir Archibald does not interfere in household arrangements. Have the Blue Room made ready for Miss Wood at once. *I* will take the responsibility,—if there is any."

On that her ladyship went away, and there was nothing for it but to carry out her orders. The Blue Room was prepared, a great fire lighted, and when I went round last thing to see all was in order for the visitor's arrival, I couldn't but think how handsome and comfortable it looked. There were candles burning brightly on the toilet-table and chimney-piece, and a fine blaze of logs on the wide hearth. I saw nothing had been overlooked, and was closing the door when my eyes fell on the bed. It was crumpled just as if someone had thrown themselves across it, and I was vexed that the housemaids should have been so careless, especially with the smart new quilt. I went round, and patted up the feathers, and smoothed the counterpane, just as the carriages drove under the window.

By and by Lady Grayburn and Miss Wood came upstairs, and knowing they had brought no maid, I went to assist in the unpacking. I was a long time in her ladyship's room, and when I'd settled her I tapped at the next door and offered to help Miss Wood. Lady Grayburn followed me almost immediately to inquire the whereabouts of some keys. She spoke very sharply, I thought, to her companion, who seemed a timid, delicate slip of a girl, with nothing noticeable about her except her hair, which was lovely, pale golden, and heaped in thick coils all round her small head.

"You will certainly be late," Lady Grayburn said. "What an age you have been, and you have not half finished unpacking yet." The young lady murmured something about there being so little time. "You have had time to sprawl on the bed instead of getting ready," was the retort, and as Miss Wood meekly denied the imputation, I looked over my shoulder at the bed, and saw there the same strange indentation I had noticed before. It made my heart beat faster, for without any reason at all I felt certain that crease must have something to do with Lady Barbara.

Miss Wood didn't go to the ball. She had supper in the school-room with the young ladies' governess, and as I heard from one of the maids that she was to sit up for Lady Grayburn, I took her some wine and sandwiches about twelve o'clock. She stayed in the school-room, with a book, till the first party came home soon after two. I'd been round the rooms with the housemaid to see the fires were kept up, and I wasn't surprised to find that queer crease back on the bed again; indeed, I sort of expected it. I said nothing to the maid, who didn't seem to have noticed anything out of the way, but I told my aunt, and though she answered sharply that I was talking nonsense, she turned quite pale, and I heard her mutter something under breath that sounded like "God help her!"

I slept badly that night, for, do what I would, the thought of that poor young lady alone in the Blue Room kept me awake and restless. I was nervous, I suppose, and once, just as I was dropping off, I started up, fancying I'd heard a scream. I opened my door and listened, but there wasn't a sound, and after waiting a bit I crept back to bed, and lay there shivering till I fell asleep.

The household wasn't astir as early as usual. Everyone was tired after the late night, and tea wasn't to be sent to the ladies till half-past nine. My aunt said nothing about the ghost, but I noticed she was fidgety, and asked almost first thing if anyone had been to Miss Wood's room. I was telling her that Martha, one of the housemaids, had just taken up the tray, when the girl came running in with a scared, white face. "For pity's sake, Mrs. Marris," she cried, "come to the Blue Room; something awful has happened!"

My aunt stopped to ask no questions. She ran straight upstairs, and as I followed, I heard her muttering to herself, "I knew it, I knew it. Oh Lord! what will my lady feel like now?"

If I live to be a hundred, I shall never forget that poor girl's face. It was just as if she'd been frozen with terror. Her eyes were wide open and fixed, and her little hands clenched in the coverlet on each side of her as she lay across the bed in the very place where that crease had been.

Of course, the whole house was aroused. Sir Archibald sent one of the grooms post-haste for the doctor, but he could do nothing when he came; Miss Wood had been dead for at least five hours.

It was a sad business. All the visitors went away as soon as possible, except Lady Grayburn, who was obliged to stay for the inquest.

In his evidence, the doctor stated death was due to failure of heart's action, occasioned possibly by some sudden shock; and though the jury did not say so in their verdict, it was an open secret that they blamed her ladyship for permitting Miss Wood to sleep in the haunted room. No one could have reproached her more bitterly than she did herself, poor lady; and if she had done wrong, she certainly suffered for it, for she never recovered from the shock of that dreadful morning, and became more or less of an invalid till her death five years later.

All this happened in 184—. It was fifty years before another woman slept in the Blue Room, and fifty years had brought with them many changes. The old Laird was gathered to his fathers, and his son, the present Sir Archibald, reigned in his stead; his sons were grown men, and Mr. Charles, the eldest, married, with a fine little boy of his own. My aunt had been dead many a year, and I was an old woman, though active and able as ever to keep the maids up to their work. They take more looking after now, I think, than in the old days before there was so much talk of education, and when young women who took service thought less of dress and more of dusting. Not but what education is a fine thing in its proper place, that is, for gentlefolk. If Miss Erristoun, now, hadn't been the clever, strong-minded young lady she is, she'd never have cleared the Blue Room of its terrible secret, and lived to make Mr. Arthur the happiest man alive.

He'd taken a great deal of notice of her when she first came in the summer to visit Mrs. Charles, and I wasn't surprised to find she was one of the guests for the opening of the shooting-season. It wasn't a regular house-party (for Sir Archibald and Lady Mertoun were away), but just half-a-dozen young ladies, friends of Mrs Charles, who was but a girl herself, and as many gentlemen that Mr. Charles and Mr. Arthur had invited. And very gay they were, what with lunches at the covert-side, and tennis-parties, and little dances got up at a few hours' notice, and sometimes of an evening they'd play hide-and-seek all over the house just as if they'd been so many children.

It surprised me at first to see Miss Erristoun, who was said to be so learned, and had held her own with all the gentlemen at Cambridge, playing with the rest like any ordinary young lady; but she seemed to enjoy the fun as much as anyone, and was always first in any amusement that was planned. I didn't wonder at Mr. Arthur's fancying her, for she was a handsome girl, tall and finely made, and carried herself like a princess. She had a wonderful head of hair, too, so long, her maid told me, it touched the ground as she sat on a chair to have it brushed. Everybody seemed to take to her, but I soon noticed it was Mr. Arthur or Mr. Calder-Maxwell she liked beat to be with.

Mr. Maxwell is a professor now, and a great man at Oxford; but then he was just an undergraduate the same as Mr. Arthur, though more studious, for he'd spend hours in the library poring over those old books full of queer black characters, that they say the wicked Lord Mertoun collected in the time of King Charles the Second. Now and then Miss Erristoun would stay indoors to help him, and it was something they found out in their studies that gave them the clue to the secret of the Blue Room.

For a long time after Miss Wood's death all mention of the ghost was strictly forbidden. Neither the Laird nor Her Ladyship could bear the slightest allusion to the subject, and the Blue Room was kept locked, except when it had to be cleaned and aired. But as the years went by the edge of the tragedy wore off and by degrees it grew to be just a story that people talked about in much the same way as they had done when I first came to the Towers; and if many believed in the mystery and speculated as to what the ghost could be, there were others who didn't hesitate to declare Miss Wood's dying in that room was a mere coincidence, and had nothing to do with supernatural agency. Miss Erristoun was one of those who held most strongly to this theory. She didn't believe a bit in ghosts, and said straight out that there wasn't any of the tales told of haunted houses which could not be traced to natural causes, if people had courage and science enough to investigate them thoroughly.

It had been very wet all that day, and the gentlemen had stayed indoors, and nothing would serve Mrs. Charles but they should all have an old-fashioned tea in my room and "talk ghosts," as she called it. They made me tell them all I knew about the Blue Room, and it was then, when everyone was discussing the story and speculating as to what the ghost could be, that Miss Erristoun spoke up. "The poor girl had heart-complaint," she finished by saying, "and she would have died the same way in any other room."

"But what about the other people who have slept there?" someone objected.

"They did not die. Old Sir Archibald came to no harm, neither did Mr. Hawksworth, nor the other man. They were healthy, and had plenty of pluck, so they saw nothing."

"They were not women," put in Mrs. Charles; "you see the ghost only appears to the weaker sex."

"That proves the story to be a mere legend," Miss Erristoun said with decision. "First it was reported that everyone who slept in the room died. Then one or two men did sleep there, and remained alive; so, the tale had to be modified, and since one woman could be proved to have died suddenly there, the fatality was represented as attaching to women only. If a girl with a sound constitution and good nerve were once to spend the night in that room, your charming family-spectre would be discredited for ever."

There was a perfect chorus of dissent. None of the ladies could agree, and most of the gentlemen doubted whether any woman's nerve would stand the ordeal. The more they argued the more Miss Erristoun persisted in her view, till at last Mrs. Charles got vexed, and cried: "Well, it is one thing to talk about it, and another to do it. Confess now, Edith, you daren't sleep in that room yourself."

"I dare and I will," she answered directly. "I don't believe in ghosts, and I am ready to stand the test I will sleep in the Blue Room to-night, if you like, and tomorrow morning you will have to confess that whatever there may be against the haunted chamber, it is not a ghost."

I think Mrs. Charles was sorry she'd spoken then, for they all took Miss Erristoun up, and the gentlemen were for laying wagers as to whether she'd see anything or not. When it was too late, she tried to laugh aside her challenge as absurd, but Miss Erristoun wouldn't be put off. She said she meant to see the thing through, and if she wasn't allowed to have a bed made up, she'd carry in her blankets and pillows, and camp out on the floor.

The others were all laughing and disputing together, but I saw Mr. Maxwell look at her very curiously. Then he drew Mr. Arthur aside, and began to talk in an undertone. I couldn't hear what he said, but Mr. Arthur answered quite short:

"It's the maddest thing I ever heard of, and I won't allow it for a moment."

"She will not ask your permission perhaps," Mr. Maxwell retorted. Then he turned to Mrs. Charles, and inquired how long it was since the Blue Room had been used, and if it was kept aired. I could speak

112

to that, and when he'd heard that there was no bedding there, but that fires were kept up regularly, he said he meant to have the first refusal of the ghost, and if he saw nothing it would be time enough for Miss Erristoun to take her turn.

Mr. Maxwell had a kind of knack of settling things, and somehow with his quiet manner always seemed to get his own way. Just before dinner he came to me with Mrs. Charles, and said it was all right, I was to get the room made ready quietly, not for all the servants to know, and he was going to sleep there.

I heard next morning that he came down to breakfast as usual. He'd had an excellent night, he said, and never slept better.

It was wet again that morning, raining "cats and dogs," but Mr. Arthur went out in it all. He'd almost quarrelled with Miss Erristoun, and was furious with Mr. Maxwell for encouraging her in her idea of testing the ghost-theory, as they called it. Those two were together in the library most of the day, and Mrs. Charles was chaffing Miss Erristoun as they went upstairs to dress, and asking her if she found the demons interesting. Yes, she said, but there was a page missing in the most exciting part of the book. They could not make head or tail of the context for some time, and then Mr. Maxwell discovered that a leaf had been cut out. They talked of nothing else all through dinner, the butler told me, and Miss Erristoun seemed so taken up with her studies, I hoped she'd forgotten about the haunted room. But she wasn't one of the sort to forget.

Later in the evening I came across her standing with Mr. Arthur in the corridor. He was talking very earnestly, and I saw her shrug her shoulders and just look up at him and smile, in a sort of way that meant she wasn't going to give in. I was slipping quietly by, for I didn't want to disturb them, when Mr. Maxwell came out of the billiard-room. "It's our game," he said; "won't you come and play the tie!"

"I'm quite ready," Miss Erristoun answered, and was turning away, when Mr. Arthur laid his hand on her arm.

"Promise me first," he urged, "promise me that much, at least."

"How tiresome you are!" she said quite pettishly. "Very well then, I promise; and now please, don't worry me anymore."

Mr. Arthur watched her go back to the billiard-room with his friend, and he gave a sort of groan. Then he caught sight of me and came along the passage. "She won't give it up," he said, and his face was quite white. "I've done all I can; I'd have telegraphed to my father, but I don't know where they'll stay in Paris, and anyway there'd be no

time to get an answer. Mrs. Marris, she's going to sleep in that d——
room, and if anything happens to her—I—" he broke off short, and
threw himself on to the window-seat, hiding his face on his folded
arms.

I could have cried for sympathy with his trouble. Mr. Arthur has
always been a favourite of mine, and I felt downright angry with Miss
Erristoun for making him so miserable just out of a bit of bravado.

"I think they are all mad," he went on presently. "Charley ought
to have stopped the whole thing at once, but Kate and the others
have talked him round. He professes to believe there's no danger, and
Maxwell has got his head full of some rubbish he has found in those
beastly books on Demonology, and he's backing her up. She won't
listen to a word I say. She told me point-blank she'd never speak to me
again if I interfered. She doesn't care a hang for me; I know that now,
but I can't help it; I—I'd give my life for her."

I did my best to comfort him, saying Miss Erristoun wouldn't
come to any harm; but it wasn't a bit of use, for I didn't believe in my
own assurances. I felt nothing but ill could come of such tempting of
Providence, and I seemed to see that other poor girl's terrible face as
it had looked when we found her dead in that wicked room. However, it is a true saying that "a wilful woman will have her way," and
we could do nothing to prevent Miss Erristoun's risking her life; but
I made up my mind to one thing, whatever other people might do, I
wasn't going to bed that night.

I'd been getting the winter-hangings into order, and the uphol-
stress had used the little *boudoir* at the end of the long corridor for her
work. I made up the fire, brought in a fresh lamp, and when the house
was quiet, I crept down and settled myself there to watch. It wasn't
ten yards from the door of the Blue Room, and over the thick carpet
I could pass without making a sound, and listen at the keyhole. Miss
Erristoun had promised Mr. Arthur she would not lock her door; it
was the one concession he'd been able to obtain from her. The ladies
went to their rooms about eleven, but Miss Erristoun stayed talking
to Mrs. Charles for nearly an hour while her maid was brushing her
hair. I saw her go to the Blue Room, and by and by Louise left her,
and all was quiet.

It must have been half-past one before I thought I heard something moving outside. I opened the door and looked out, and there
was Mr. Arthur standing in the passage. He gave a start when he saw
me. "You are sitting up," he said, coming into the room; "then you do

believe there is evil work on hand tonight? The others have gone to bed, but I can't rest; it's no use my trying to sleep. I meant to stay in the smoking-room, but it is so far away; I couldn't hear there even if she called for help. I've listened at the door; there isn't a sound. Can't you go in and see if it's all right? Oh, Marris, if she should—"

I knew what he meant, but I wasn't going to admit *that* possible—yet. "I can't go into a lady's room without any reason," I said; "but I've been to the door every few minutes for the last hour and more. It wasn't till half-past twelve that Miss Erristoun stopped moving about, and I don't believe, Mr. Arthur, that God will let harm come to her, without giving those that care for her some warning. I mean to keep on listening, and if there's the least hint of anything wrong, why I'll go to her at once, and you are at hand here to help."

I talked to him a bit more till he seemed more reasonable, and then we sat there waiting, hardly speaking a word except when, from time to time, I went outside to listen. The house was deathly quiet; there was something terrible, I thought, in the stillness; not a sign of life anywhere save just in the little *boudoir*, where Mr. Arthur paced up and down, or sat with a strained look on his face, watching the door.

As three o'clock struck, I went out again. There is a window in the corridor, angle for angle with the *boudoir* door. As I passed, someone stepped from behind the curtains and a voice whispered: "Don't be frightened Mrs. Marris; it is only me, Calder-Maxwell. Mr. Arthur is there, isn't he?" He pushed open the *boudoir* door. "May I come in?" he said softly. "I guessed you'd be about, Mertoun. I'm not at all afraid myself, but if there is anything in that little legend, it is as well for some of us to be on hand. It was a good idea of yours to get Mrs. Marris to keep watch with you."

Mr. Arthur looked at him as black as thunder. "If you didn't know there was something in it," he said, "you wouldn't be here now; and knowing that, you're nothing less than a blackguard for egging that girl on to risk her life, for the sake of trying to prove your insane theories. You are no friend of mine after this, and I'll never willingly see you or speak to you again."

I was fairly frightened at his words, and for how Mr. Maxwell might take them; but he just smiled, and lighted a cigarette, quite cool and quiet.

"I'm not going to quarrel with you, old chap," he said. "You're a bit on the strain tonight, and when a man has nerves, he mustn't be held responsible for all his words." Then he turned to me. "You're a sensible woman, Mrs. Marris, and a brave one too, I fancy. If I stay here with Mr. Arthur, will you keep close outside Miss Erristoun's door? She may talk in her sleep quietly; that's of no consequence; but if she should cry out, go in at once, *at once,* you understand; we shall hear you, and follow immediately."

At that Mr. Arthur was on his feet. "You know more than you pretend," he cried. "You slept in that room last night. By Heaven, if you've played any trick on her I'll—"

Mr. Maxwell held the door open. "Will you go, please, Mrs. Marris?" he said in his quiet way. "Mertoun, don't be a d—— fool."

I went as he told me, and I give you my word I was all ears, for I felt certain Mr. Maxwell knew more than we did, and that he expected something to happen.

It seemed like hours, though I know now it could not have been more than a quarter of that time, before I could be positive someone was moving behind that closed door.

At first, I thought it was only my own heart, which was beating against my ribs like a hammer; but soon I could distinguish footsteps, and a sort of murmur like someone speaking continuously, but very low. Then a voice (it was Miss Erristoun's this time) said, "No, it is impossible; I am dreaming, I must be dreaming." There was a kind of rustling as though she were moving quickly across the floor. I had my fingers on the handle, but I seemed as if I'd lost power to stir; I could only wait for what might come next.

Suddenly she began to say something out loud. I could not make out the words, which didn't sound like English, but almost directly she stopped short. "I can't remember any more," she cried in a troubled tone.

"What shall I do? I can't—"

There was a pause. Then—"No, *no!*" she shrieked. "Oh, Arthur, Arthur!"

At that my strength came back to me, and I flung open the door.

There was a night-lamp burning on the table, and the room was quite light. Miss Erristoun was standing by the bed; she seemed to have backed up against it; her hands were down at her sides, her fingers clutching at the quilt. Her face was white as a sheet, and her eyes staring wide with terror, as well they might—I know I never had such a shock in my life, for if it was my last word, I swear there was a man standing close in front of her. He turned and looked at me as I opened the door, and I saw his face as plain as I did hers. He was young and very handsome, and his eyes shone like an animal's when you see them in the dark.

"Arthur!" Miss Erristoun gasped again, and I saw she was fainting. I sprang forward, and caught her by the shoulders just as she was falling back on to the bed.

It was all over in a second. Mr. Arthur had her in his arms, and when I looked up there were only us four in the room, for Mr. Maxwell had followed on Mr. Arthur's heels, and was kneeling beside me with his fingers on Miss Erristoun's pulse. "It's only a faint," he said, "she'll come round directly. Better take her out of this at once; here's a dressing-gown." He threw the wrapper round her, and would have helped to raise her, but Mr. Arthur needed no assistance. He lifted Miss Erristoun as if she'd been a baby, and carried her straight to the *boudoir*. He laid her on the couch and knelt beside her, chafing her hands. "Get the brandy out of the smoking room, Maxwell," he said. "Mrs. Marris, have you any salt handy?"

I always carry a bottle in my pocket, so I gave it to him, before I ran after Mr. Maxwell, who had lighted a candle, and was going for the brandy. "Shall I wake Mr. Charles and the servants?" I cried. "He'll be hiding somewhere, but he hasn't had time to get out of the house yet."

He looked as if he thought I was crazed. "He—who?" he asked.

"The man," I said; "there was a man in Miss Erristoun's room. I'll call up Soames and Robert."

"You'll do nothing of the sort," he said sharply. "There was no man in that room."

"There was," I retorted, "for I saw him; and a great powerful man too. Someone ought to go for the police before he has time to get off."

Mr. Maxwell was always an odd sort of gentleman, but I didn't know what to make of the way he behaved then. He just leaned against the wall, and laughed till the tears came into his eyes.

"It is no laughing matter that I can see," I told him quite short, for I was angry at his treating the matter so lightly; "and I consider it no more than my duty to let Mr. Charles know that there's a burglar on the premises."

He grew grave at once then. "I beg your pardon, Mrs. Marris," he said seriously; "but I couldn't help smiling at the idea of the police. The vicar would be more to the point, all things considered. You really must not think of rousing the household; it might do Miss Erristoun a great injury, and could in no case be of the slightest use. Don't you understand? It was not a man at all you saw, it was an—well, it was what haunts the Blue Room."

Then he ran downstairs leaving me fairly dazed, for I'd made so sure what I'd seen was a real man, that I'd clean forgotten all about the ghost.

Miss Erristoun wasn't long regaining consciousness. She swallowed the brandy we gave her like a lamb, and sat up bravely, though she started at every sound, and kept her hand in Mr. Arthur's like a frightened child. It was strange, seeing how independent and stand-off she'd been with him before, but she seemed all the sweeter for the change. It was as if they'd come to an understanding without any words; and, indeed, he must have known she had eared for him all along, when she called out his name in her terror.

As soon as she'd recovered herself a little, Mr. Maxwell began asking questions. Mr. Arthur would have stopped him, but he insisted that it was of the greatest importance to hear everything while the impression was fresh; and when she had got over the first effort, Miss Erristoun seemed to find relief in telling her experience. She sat there with one hand in Mr. Arthur's while she spoke, and Mr. Maxwell wrote down what she said in his pocketbook.

She told us she went to bed quite easy, for she wasn't the least nervous, and being tired she soon dropped off to sleep. Then she had a sort of dream, I suppose, for she thought she was in the same room, only differently furnished, all but the bed. She described exactly how everything was arranged. She had the strangest feeling too, that she was not herself but someone else, and that she was going to do something,—something that must be done, though she was frightened to death all the time, and kept stopping to listen at the inner door, expecting someone would hear her moving about and call out for her to go to them. That in itself was queer, for there was nobody sleeping in the adjoining room.

In her dream, she went on to say, she saw a curious little silver brazier, one that stands in a cabinet in the picture-gallery (a fine example of *cinque cento* work, I think I've heard my lady call it), and this she remembered holding in her hands a long time, before she set it on a little table beside the bed. Now the bed in the Blue Boom is very handsome, richly carved on the cornice and frame, and especially on the posts, which are a foot square at the base and covered with relief-work in a design of fruit and flowers. Miss Erristoun said she went to the left-hand post at the foot, and after passing her hand over the carving, she seemed to touch a spring in one of the centre flowers, and the panel fell outwards like a lid, disclosing a secret cupboard out of which she took some papers and a box. She seemed to know what to do with the papers, though she couldn't tell us what was written on them; and she had a distinct recollection of taking a *pastille* from the box, and lighting it in the silver brazier. The smoke curled up and seemed to fill the whole room with a heavy perfume, and the next thing she remembered was that she awoke to find herself standing in the middle of the floor, and—what I had seen when I opened the door was there.

She turned quite white when she came to that part of the story, and shuddered. "I couldn't believe it," she said; "I tried to think I was still dreaming, but I wasn't, I wasn't. It was real, and it was there, and—oh, it was horrible!"

She hid her face against Mr. Arthur's shoulder. Mr. Maxwell sat, pencil in hand, staring at her. "I was right then," he said. "I felt sure I was; but it seemed incredible."

"It is incredible," said Miss Erristoun; "but it is true, frightfully true. When I realised that I was awake, that it was actually real, I tried to remember the charge, you know, out of the office of exorcism, but I couldn't get through it. The words went out of my head; I felt my will-power failing; I was paralysed, as though I could make no effort to help myself and then—then I—," she looked at Mr. Arthur and blushed all over her face and neck. "I thought of you, and I called—I had a feeling that you would save me."

Mr. Arthur made no more ado about us than if we'd been a couple of dummies. He just put his arms round her and kissed her, while Mr. Maxwell and I looked the other way.

After a bit, Mr. Maxwell said: "One more question, please; what was it like?"

She answered after thinking for a minute. "It was like a man, tall and very handsome. I have an impression that its eyes were blue and very bright." Mr. Maxwell looked at me inquiringly, and I nodded. "And dressed!" he asked. She began to laugh almost hysterically. "It sounds too insane for words, but I think—I am almost positive it wore ordinary evening dress."

"It is impossible," Mr. Arthur cried. "You were dreaming the whole time, that proves it."

"It doesn't," Mr. Maxwell contradicted. "They usually appeared in the costume of the day. You'll find that stated particularly both by Scott and Glanvil; Sprenger gives an instance too. Besides, Mrs. Marris thought it was a burglar, which argues that the—the manifestation was objective, and presented no striking peculiarity in the way of clothing."

"What?" Miss Erristoun exclaimed.

"You saw it too?" I told her exactly what I had seen. My description tallied with hers in everything, but the white shirt and tie, which from my position at the door I naturally should not be able to see.

Mr. Maxwell snapped the elastic round his note-book. For a long time, he sat silently staring at the fire. "It is almost past belief," he said at last, speaking half to himself, "that such a thing could happen at the end of the nineteenth century, in these scientific rationalistic times that we think such a lot about, we, who look down from our superior intellectual height on the benighted superstitions of the Middle Ages." He gave an odd little laugh. "I'd like to get to the bottom of this business. I have a theory, and in the interest of psychical research and common humanity, I'd like to work it out Miss Erristoun, you ought, I know, to have rest and quiet, and it is almost morning; but will you grant me one request. Before you are overwhelmed with questions, before you are made to relate your experience till the impression of tonight's adventure loses edge and clearness, will you go with Mertoun and myself to the Blue Room, and try to find the secret panel?"

"She shall never set foot inside that door again," Mr. Arthur began hotly, but Miss Erristoun laid a restraining hand on his arm.

"Wait a moment, dear," she said gently; "let us hear Mr. Maxwell's reasons. Do you think," she went on, "that my dream had a foundation in fact; that something connected with that dreadful thing is really concealed about the room?"

"I think," he answered, "that you hold the clue to the mystery, and I believe, could you repeat the action of your dream, and open the secret panel, you might remove for ever the legacy of one woman's reckless folly. Only if it is to be done at all, it must be soon, before the impression has had time to fade."

"It shall be done now," she answered; "I am quite myself again. Feel my pulse; my nerves are perfectly steady."

Mr. Arthur broke out into angry protestations. She had gone through more than enough for one night, he said, and he wouldn't have her health sacrificed to Maxwell's whims.

I have always thought Miss Erristoun handsome, but never, not even on her wedding-day, did she look so beautiful as then when she stood up in her heavy white wrapper, with all her splendid hair loose on her shoulders.

"Listen," she said; "if God gives us a plain work to do, we must do it at any cost. Last night I didn't believe in anything I could not understand. I was so full of pride in my own courage and common-sense, that I wasn't afraid to sleep in that room and prove the ghost was all superstitious nonsense. I have learned there are forces of which I know nothing, and against which my strength was utter weakness. God took care of me, and sent help in time; and if He has opened a way by which I may save other women from the danger I escaped, I should be worse than ungrateful were I to shirk the task. Bring the lamp, Mr. Maxwell, and let us do what we can." Then she put both hands on Mr. Arthur's shoulders. "Why are you troubled?" she said sweetly. "You will be with me, and how can I be afraid?"

It never strikes me as strange now that burglaries and things can go on in a big house at night, and not a soul one whit the wiser. There were five people sleeping in the rooms on that corridor while we tramped up and down without disturbing one of them. Not but what we went as quietly as we could, for Mr. Maxwell made it clear that the less was known about the actual facts, the better. He went first, carrying the lamp, and we followed. Miss Erristoun shivered as her eyes fell on the bed, across which that dreadful crease showed plain, and I knew she was thinking of what might have been, had help not been at hand.

Just for a minute she faltered, then she went bravely on, and began feeling over the carved woodwork for the spring of the secret panel. Mr. Maxwell held the lamp close, but there was nothing to show any difference between that bit of carving and the other three posts. For full ten minutes she tried, and so did the gentlemen, and it seemed as though the dream would turn out a delusion after all, when all at once Miss Erristoun cried, "I have found it," and with a little jerk, the square of wood fell forward, and there was the cupboard just as she had described it to us.

It was Mr. Maxwell who took out the things, for Mr. Arthur wouldn't let Miss Erristoun touch them. There were a roll of papers and a little silver box. At the sight of the box she gave a sort of cry; "That is it," she said, and covered her face with her hands.

Mr. Maxwell lifted the lid, and emptied out two or three *pastilles*. Then he unfolded the papers, and before he had fairly glanced at the sheet of parchment covered with queer black characters, he cried, "I knew it, I knew it! It *is* the missing leaf." He seemed quite wild with excitement.

"Come along," he said. "Bring the light, Mertoun; I always said it was no ghost, and now the whole thing is as clear as daylight. You see," he went on, as we gathered round the table in the *boudoir*, "so much depended on there being an heir. That was the chief cause of the endless quarrels between old Lord Mertoun and Barbara. He had never approved of the marriage, and was for ever reproaching the poor woman with having failed in the first duty of an only son's wife. His will shows that he did not leave her a farthing in event of her husband dying without issue. Then the feud with the Protestant branch of the family was very bitter, and the Sir Archibald of that day had three boys, he having married (about the same time as his cousin) Lady Mary Sarum, who had been Barbara's rival at Court and whom Barbara very naturally hated. So, when the doctors pronounced Dennis Mertoun to be dying of consumption, his wife got desperate, and had recourse to black magic.

"It is well known that the old man's collection of works on Demonology was the most complete in Europe. Lady Barbara must have had access to the books, and it was she who cut out this leaf. Probably Lord Mertoun discovered the theft and drew his own conclusions. That would account for his refusal to admit her body to the family vault. The Mertouns were staunch Romanists, and it is one of the deadly sins, you know, meddling with sorcery. Well, Barbara contrived to procure the *pastilles*, and she worked out the spell according to the directions given here, and then—Good God! Mertoun, what have you done?"

For before anyone could interfere to check him, Mr. Arthur had swept papers, box, *pastilles*, and all off the table and flung them into the fire. The thick parchment curled and shrivelled on the hot coals, and a queer, faint smell like incense spread heavily through the room. Mr. Arthur stepped to the window and threw the casement wide open. Day was breaking, and a sweet fresh wind swept in from the east which was all rosy with the glow of the rising sun.

"It is a nasty story," he said; "and if there be any truth in it, for the credit of the family and the name of a dead woman, let it rest for ever. We will keep our own counsel about tonight's work. It is enough for others to know that the spell of the Blue Room is broken, since a brave, pure-minded girl has dared to face its unknown mystery and has laid the ghost."

Mr. Calder-Maxwell considered a moment. "I believe you are right," he said, presently, with an air of resignation. "I agree to your proposition, and I surrender my chance of world-wide celebrity among the votaries of Psychical Research; but I *do* wish, Mertoun, you would call things by their proper names. It was *not* a ghost It was an—"

But as I said, all I can remember now of the word he used is, that it somehow put me in mind of poultry-rearing.

Note.—The reader will observe that the worthy Mrs. Marris, though no student of Sprenger, unconsciously discerned the root-affinity of the incubator of the hen-yard and the incubus of the Malleus Maleficarum.

LEONAUR

ALSO FROM LEONAUR
AVAILABLE IN SOFTCOVER OR HARDCOVER WITH DUST JACKET

MR MUKERJI'S GHOSTS *by S. Mukerji*—Supernatural tales from the British Raj period by India's Ghost story collector.

KIPLINGS GHOSTS *by Rudyard Kipling*—Twelve stories of Ghosts, Hauntings, Curses, Werewolves & Magic.

THE COLLECTED SUPERNATURAL AND WEIRD FICTION OF WASHINGTON IRVING: VOLUME 1 *by Washington Irving*—Including one novel 'A History of New York', and nine short stories of the Strange and Unusual.

THE COLLECTED SUPERNATURAL AND WEIRD FICTION OF WASHINGTON IRVING: VOLUME 2 *by Washington Irving*—Including three novelettes 'The Legend of the Sleepy Hollow', 'Dolph Heyliger', 'The Adventure of the Black Fisherman' and thirty-two short stories of the Strange and Unusual.

THE COLLECTED SUPERNATURAL AND WEIRD FICTION OF JOHN KENDRICK BANGS: VOLUME 1 *by John Kendrick Bangs*—Including one novel 'Toppleton's Client or A Spirit in Exile', and ten short stories of the Strange and Unusual.

THE COLLECTED SUPERNATURAL AND WEIRD FICTION OF JOHN KENDRICK BANGS: VOLUME 2 *by John Kendrick Bangs*—Including four novellas 'A House-Boat on the Styx', 'The Pursuit of the House-Boat', 'The Enchanted Typewriter' and 'Mr. Munchausen' of the Strange and Unusual.

THE COLLECTED SUPERNATURAL AND WEIRD FICTION OF JOHN KENDRICK BANGS: VOLUME 3 *by John Kendrick Bangs*—Including twor novellas 'Olympian Nights', 'Roger Camerden: A Strange Story', and ten short stories of the Strange and Unusual.

THE COLLECTED SUPERNATURAL AND WEIRD FICTION OF MARY SHELLEY: VOLUME 1 *by Mary Shelley*—Including one novel 'Frankenstein or the Modern Prometheus', and fourteen short stories of the Strange and Unusual.

THE COLLECTED SUPERNATURAL AND WEIRD FICTION OF MARY SHELLEY: VOLUME 2 *by Mary Shelley*—Including one novel 'The Last Man', and three short stories of the Strange and Unusual.

THE COLLECTED SUPERNATURAL AND WEIRD FICTION OF AMELIA B. EDWARDS *by Amelia B. Edwards*—Contains two novelettes 'Monsieur Maurice', and 'The Discovery of the Treasure Isles', one ballad 'A Legend of Boisguilbert' and seventeen short stories to cill the blood.

LEONAUR

ALSO FROM LEONAUR
AVAILABLE IN SOFTCOVER OR HARDCOVER WITH DUST JACKET

THE COLLECTED SCIENCE FICTION AND FANTASY OF STANLEY G. WEINBAUM 1—INTERPLANETARY ODYSSEYS *by Stanley G. Weinbaum*—Classic Tales of Interplanetary Adventure Including: A Martian Odyssey, its Sequel Valley of Dreams, the Complete 'Ham' Hammond Stories and Others.

THE COLLECTED SCIENCE FICTION AND FANTASY OF STANLEY G. WEINBAUM 2—OTHER EARTHS *by Stanley G. Weinbaum*—Classic Futuristic Tales Including: *Dawn of Flame* & its Sequel The Black Flame, plus The Revolution of 1960 & Others.

THE COLLECTED SCIENCE FICTION AND FANTASY OF STANLEY G. WEINBAUM 3—STRANGE GENIUS *by Stanley G. Weinbaum*—Classic Tales of the Human Mind at Work Including the Complete Novel The New Adam, the 'van Manderpootz' Stories and Others.

THE COLLECTED SCIENCE FICTION AND FANTASY OF STANLEY G. WEINBAUM 4—THE BLACK HEART *by Stanley G. Weinbaum*—Classic Strange Tales Including: the Complete Novel The Dark Other, Plus Proteus Island and Others.

THE COLLECTED SCIENCE FICTION & FANTASY OF JACK LONDON 1—BEFORE ADAM & OTHER STORIES *by Jack London*—included in this Volume Before Adam The Scarlet Plague A Relic of the Pliocene When the World Was Young The Red One Planchette A Thousand Deaths Goliah A Curious Fragment The Rejuvenation of Major Rathbone.

THE COLLECTED SCIENCE FICTION & FANTASY OF JACK LONDON 2—THE IRON HEEL & OTHER STORIES *by Jack London*—included in this Volume The Iron Heel The Enemy of All the World The Shadow and the Flash The Strength of the Strong The Unparalleled Invasion The Dream of Debs.

THE COLLECTED SCIENCE FICTION & FANTASY OF JACK LONDON 3—THE STAR ROVER & OTHER STORIES *by Jack London*—included in this Volume The Star Rover The Minions of Midas The Eternity of Forms The Man With the Gash.

www.ingramcontent.com/pod-product-compliance
Lightning Source LLC
Chambersburg PA
CBHW050308260626
47156CB00005B/1706